The Quiet Game

by

Ash Warren

**A Penelope Middleton
Japanese Murder Mystery**

For Linda and Geoffrey

Chapter 1

A Shadow on the Moon

For more than a thousand years, there has been a tradition of moon viewing in Japan. The most common nights for this practice were naturally those of the full moon, occasions where friends gathered to pass the night together until dawn, enjoying the moonlit hours drinking *sake* and writing poems. Unlike now, since ancient times the passage of time had also been marked using the old lunar calendar, and according to this, the most important moon of the year fell on the eighteenth night of the eighth month, which this year was the tenth day of September. This was the great harvest moon in Japan and a special time to celebrate the rice harvest and enjoy the many autumn delicacies which were becoming available.

Each year Professor Penelope Middleton and her friend Dr. Fei Chen were invited by Chief Inspector Yamashita to a moon viewing party held at the house of Ryonosuke Suwamoto, who at one time had been the principal conductor of the Tokyo Philharmonic Orchestra and an old family friend of the Yamashita's. Suwamoto-san had been at school with the chief inspector's late father, so Yamashita had known the now elderly musician since boyhood, and they had always used this occasion as their main means of staying in touch over the years.

Suwamoto lived in an elegant old wooden home in the hills above Kamakura which was blessed with a magnificent formal Japanese garden, including a pond stocked with shimmering golden carp, and, for this occasion each year, small paper lanterns floating on the dark surface for the celebration of the *chushu-no meigetsu,* or the great mid-autumn moon.

Most of the women present dressed in *kimono* for this event, and Penelope usually brought a gift of rice dumplings called *tsukimi dango,* which she made herself and which were traditional at this time of year, whereas Yamashita supplied a large bottle of very good *sake*, without which a moon viewing party would be incomplete on any level.

On arrival this year Suwamoto greeted them warmly at the door, dressed in a beautiful dark men's *kimono,* and escorted them through the house to the garden where the other guests were mingling and admiring the huge glowing moon that was just then easing itself above the treetops. Much to everyone's delight tonight, the sky was clear and full of stars, making the evening even more memorable, especially for those who had been here on less clement occasions.

"So Eiji!" said Suwamoto with a wry smile and looking him up and down, "Once again, I see the ladies here have made an effort, but not you, it seems…" a comment on the fact that the chief inspector was wearing a casual jacket and open-necked shirt rather than something more traditional.

"I made an effort to bring this. That should be enough, I think," said Yamashita-san, holding up the large bottle of sake and offering it to their host.

Suwamoto nodded and accepted the bottle.

"You're right….it is. I forgive you," he said with a laugh. "But you girls, my God, you look more beautiful every year…" he said to Penelope and Fei, who both gave him a slight bow.

Fei, though, was having none of his faux compliments.

"First of all," she said, in her usual feisty way, "As a doctor, I recommend you see an optometrist as soon as possible, as there is clearly something wrong with your eyes or perhaps your sanity throwing compliments like that at middle-aged women like us. Secondly, I would never get into this contraption for anyone but you…" she smiled, holding her long sleeves apart and giving him a little twirl in her kimono. "But if it weren't for Penny-*sensei*, it would have taken about a month to get ready."

Fei, it was true, hated formality of any kind, but she had gradually been overcome by the romance of these evenings and had finally given in to Penelope's pleadings and started to wear *kimono*. Penelope, her best friend and neighbor of many years, was fortunately an old hand at the tea ceremony and had chests full of *kimono* for her to choose from.

Penelope herself could dress in *kimono* in about half an hour flat, which was a near-professional speed, so she took charge of her friend and dressed her as well. Tonight they were both wearing *kimono* with a maple leaf pattern, as were many of the other women there that evening to mark the season, even though the leaves were still a few months away from showing their beautiful colors in Kamakura yet.

Penelope had her shoulder-length silver hair swept up in an elegant bun, and wore her half-glasses on a long silver chain around her neck, as she had found to her annoyance that she was fairly blind without them these days. In the days before she had retired as a professor of Japanese literature at the nearby Hassei university, she had never worn glasses at all, but now, just a few years later, she found she could not even cut vegetables for dinner properly without them. Apart from her eyes, which were a sharp blue like the sky and which missed nothing, she was still in perfect health, had a slender figure, and could walk distances that would have daunted a woman half her age.

"Thank you for having us again, Ryonosuke-san," she commented to her host. "It's always so beautiful here… And don't listen to Fei, she secretly loves to wear *kimono*, she just won't tell anybody," she nodded at her friend who was now making her way across the garden, stepping carefully on the flag-stoned path towards a little ornamental bridge across the pond in her wooden *zori* sandals and having a bit of difficulty trying to maintain her balance in the unfamiliar footwear.

Suwamoto-san watched her slightly teetering progress across the moonlit garden with some amusement.

"Well, so long as she doesn't fall into the pond, then you have done wonders training her, Penny-*sensei*," he smiled, and ran his hands through his long silver mane of hair.

The sound of the *jushichigen koto*, the seventeen-string Japanese zither or 'bass koto' drifted from the open doors of the house across the garden, and Penelope gave a nod to the koto-player, Karimoto-san, a nice young woman whom she had known for a number of years in the music department of her old university. Accompanied by songs that had been composed centuries before for such evenings, she walked over to join Fei and the other guests sitting on little stools in the garden, admiring the moon and chatting.

She knew a lot of the people from previous gatherings, and so she was soon accosted by several old friends, many of whom she had not met since the last year.

"I'm so pleased the weather is better this year," said Inaba-san, an older woman and a cousin of Suwamoto's whom she met here every year. "We've been pretty unlucky in the past. But tonight… it's just perfect, isn't it," she smiled, looking up at the sky.

"Yes, it certainly is. I don't think it's been this good for several years. There isn't a cloud," said Penelope, sitting down on an empty stool next to her.

Fei came over and tugged her sleeve. "Do you think they are ever going to serve the drinks? I'm parched. And starving. I swear wearing this thing makes me hungry. Like I want to burst out of it."

Penelope and Inaba-san laughed.

"I think it suits you, Fei-san. And Penelope. Some foreigners just look so good in *kimono*…."

Fei wagged her finger. "*She's* foreign. I was born here."

"That's true. I'm sorry." said Inaba-san.

"Don't worry about her," said Penelope. "Fei is the most Chinese person I know. Apart from her aunt, of course…."

"No one is more Chinese than Auntie," said Fei, referring to the redoubtable Mrs. Chen, the elderly aunt she lived with in the house next door to Penelope. "She's more Chinese than Confucius."

"Yes, I've met her several times you know, it's true!" said Inaba-san with a laugh. "Oh, here is Yamashita-san. Fei-san wants a drink. Me too, actually. Since you have on those nice easy shoes, we have decided you're our waiter for the night."

Yamashita-san bowed. "That's why I wear them. So I can get to the bar faster," he smiled, and turning on his heel, he went back to the house to fetch some *sake* and champagne.

Penelope stood up and wandered over to talk to some other people she had just seen, when she felt someone touch her on the arm.

"Penny-*sensei*? Do you remember me?"

It was a tall, slender woman wearing a dark, russet-colored *kimono* tied with a bright yellow *obi* that looked almost white in the moonlight. She was perhaps about forty years old and was wearing her hair loose so that it fell past her shoulders. She had a rather thin, strained face, but it was lit up by her luminous dark eyes, which looked somehow as if they had not been a stranger to some great sadness in her past.

"Oh, hello…" said Penelope, who had no idea whom she was addressing, but was hoping the woman would help her out.

"It's me. Mari. Mari Setouchi. I'm sure you have no idea who I am, I'm sorry. I took your Japanese literature class once when I was a student. It must be well over twenty years ago now….."

Penelope bowed politely and looked at her carefully, but still had no memory.

"Forgive me, Setouchi-san. I've had so many students over the years, and I have trouble remembering what my cats are called these days. It's nice to see an old student, though. How are you?"

Mari smiled and looked happy.

8

"I'm fine. It's so nice to see you too, after all these years. I'm not surprised you don't remember me, I wasn't even a literature major. I studied painting, actually."

Penelope nodded, and then a memory of her name rang a bell in her mind.

"You're not *the* Mari Setouchi... the artist Mari Setouchi... are you?"

The woman nodded. "I'm afraid that's me," she said.

Penelope remembered her now, but not from the university. She had seen her name several times in the newspapers and on television over the years. She was widely known as one of Japan's most famous contemporary painters, and lived in Kamakura, where she had her studio and also where she frequently held exhibitions.

"Ah, now I remember," said Penelope. "How do you know Suwamoto-san?"

"Ryonosuke? Oh, he's been to my exhibitions. I think he's even bought a couple of my paintings, maybe they're hanging up somewhere inside. Hopefully not in his closet anyway. This is the first time he has invited me here, though."

"Do you still live in Kamakura?"

"Yes, we do. My niece and I live not too far away, about a ten-minute walk."

"Ah," said Penelope. "I always envy people who live up here in the hills. It's such a nice area. Lots of big old homes like this one, too."

"Yes, I know what you mean. In my line of work you tend to need a bit of space for a studio and whatnot. So I was kind of forced to look around up here. I was lucky to find something, though it took a bit of work to convert. You know these old Japanese-style homes are not big on natural light."

"That's true. A lot of them are as dark as tombs. Is your niece here too?

Mari looked around. "Yes, there she is. Suzume!" she called, and a girl who was crouching next to the pond watching the carp looked up and came over to join them.

"Su-chan, I want you to meet my old teacher from university. This is Middleton-*sensei*," she said, gesturing towards Penelope.

The girl gave a small bow. She was probably about eighteen years old and was dressed in a light blue kimono with a butterfly pattern. She was also strikingly beautiful. Penelope thought she could see a lot of her aunt in her face, but her eyes were far more luminous and dreamy.

"Hello. I'm Suzume," she said with a pretty smile.

Penelope introduced herself.

"Are you in high school?" she asked.

Suzume nodded. "I just graduated, thank heavens."

"In Kamakura?"

"Yes." She named one of the better schools in the area, which Penelope knew.

"That's a good school. Are you planning to go on to university next year?" Penelope asked.

Suzume looked down, and Penelope wondered if she had touched on a painful subject.

"She does have plans, but not university, unfortunately. At least not this year anyway." said her aunt. "I've been trying to persuade her, but....."

"Well, not everyone has to go to university," remarked Penelope. "Far too many do, in my opinion, when they should be doing something else. What are you thinking about? Anything in particular?"

Suzume gave a shy smile.

"She wants to be a professional *shogi* player," said her aunt. "She's pretty good too. And it's all she thinks about, I'm afraid."

"Well, you've come to the right place. Have you met Dr. Chen?"

Suzume shook her head.

"Well, there are a few other victims of the *shogi* bug here tonight. Like Fei-san over there. And not to mention the dashing Chief Inspector Yamashita, who seems to have forgotten to bring me a drink," she gestured at the chief inspector, who was standing talking to someone behind them.

Suzume looked over at Fei. "Oh, is that Fei Chen? I've seen pictures of her. In the *shogi* magazines. She's quite a well-known player."

"That's what she tells people too. Let me introduce you."

Although Penelope did not play the game of *shogi*, otherwise known as Japanese chess, it was very much a part of her life because of Fei and Yamashita-san, who both played it at a very high level, particularly Fei. At least once a month, they had dinner and *shogi* either at her house or at Fei's, where her aunt would usually provide a huge Chinese meal that would easily have re-supplied an army regiment.

She escorted Suzume and her aunt over to where Fei was sitting and introduced them.

"Fei, this is Suzume. She plays *shogi*. I thought you might like to meet her."

Fei looked up and smiled, and Suzume bowed politely.

"Oh… you're too pretty to play *shogi*. It would help if you looked more like a mean old dragon like me," said Fei.

Suzume blushed, and Penelope asked Mari if she would like to hear the *koto* being played with her, mainly to let Suzume and Fei have a chance to talk.

"Sure," said Mari. "I love the *koto*."

The two women walked back to the house and stood watching Karimoto-san play for a while.

"Oh!" said Mari, pointing to a painting on the far wall behind the musician. "That's one of mine I was telling you about."

"Really? Let's go and have a look," said Penelope.

They slipped off their *zori* and stepped onto the little wooden verandah and into the house.

The painting was quite large, taking up nearly half the wall, and showed a woman's naked body surrounded by flames. The woman's mouth was open, seemingly in surprise rather than pain, as if she barely noticed the fire that seemed to be engulfing her.

"That's amazing," said Penelope. "Wherever did you get the idea?"

Mari smiled. "It's called *Woman on Fire* - I guess that's fairly obvious. I've been working with the fire motif for some time now, it's something I find interesting, you know, the cleansing power of fire, as well as the destructive side. So recently, a lot of my work features it…."

"Well, it's very impressive. I like it."

"That's kind of you. I think the jury is still out, though," said Mari modestly. "Are you still teaching at Hassei?"

"No, I retired several years ago, but I'm still writing stuff. No teaching though, thank heavens," said Penelope. "How did your niece get interested in *shogi*? That game seems to follow me around for some reason, not that I have much of an idea how to play it. Fei tried to teach me a few times, but I think she decided I was too stupid. She's probably right."

Mari smiled. "I think she just picked it up at school, but she has been playing at a pretty high level for years now. I think she must have *shogi* in her DNA. Maybe like I have art. My dad wanted to be an art teacher when he was in high school, but he ended up farming. I think that's where I got it from. That's when he wasn't out hunting bears with my uncle when he was alive. We used to live in Akita, and my sister still does. She has a house full of guns, poor woman."

The two women reminisced for a while, and then they gathered in the garden and, since the host wanted to make it as authentic a moon viewing as possible, some of those assembled read poems they had composed for the occasion, and others read some of the Chinese classics. As someone with her former job, Penelope was expected to contribute, and this evening she read an old Chinese poem by Li Bai, entitled 'Drinking Alone Under the Moon"

Among the blossoms waits a jug of wine.
I pour myself a drink, no loved one near.
Raising my cup, I invite the bright moon
and turn to my shadow.
We are now three.
But the moon doesn't understand drinking,
And my shadow follows my body like a slave.
For a time moon and shadow will be my companions,
a passing joy that should last through the spring.
I sing and the moon just wavers in the sky;

13

I dance and my shadow whips around like mad.
While lucid still, we have such fun together!
But stumbling drunk, each staggers off alone.
Bound forever, relentless we roam:
reunited at last
on the distant river of stars.

Much later, as the moon began to slip beneath the western hills behind the house, the party began to break up. Nearly everyone had drunk too much, so taxis were called, and the guests departed for home with promises to return again next year.

Chief Inspector Yamashita was one of the last to leave, and about twenty minutes later, his taxi deposited him in front of his old home near Meigetsu-in temple in the Kita-Kamakura area.

He also had drunk too much, as was usual whenever he visited Suwamoto-san, and had a moment of difficulty finding the correct key for the lock and getting inside.

As he closed the door behind him, he had no idea what was waiting for him. The ghost of a long-unsolved crime, a series of bloody events that had baffled the best minds in the police for many years, was about to awaken from its long slumber.

As he put his keys in the little bronze bowl next to the door, he heard the telephone in his living room begin to ring.

As a police officer, the only reason someone would call him at home at this hour was if it was an emergency. Thinking it must be either his office at the Kamakura Police

14

station or some family problem, he walked briskly into the living room and picked up the receiver.

"Yamashita," he said curtly.

There was no reply at all for several seconds on the other end of the line... and then he distinctly heard someone breathing heavily and slowly.

"Yamashita," he repeated.

The breathing continued. Thinking this must be a prank or a wrong number, he was just about to hang up when he heard a harsh voice that sounded like someone speaking in a loud whisper. The words and that cold, somehow inhuman voice sent a chill straight down the back of his neck.

"Check your mailbox," it hissed.

Chapter 2

The Return

Dear Little Policemen,

I'm back!

It's been such a long time, let's see… is it really eighteen years?
How time flies.
I hope you missed me anyway.
It appears I am still free to roam the earth, but…never mind. I'm
going to give you another chance to stop my fun, which is rather generous
of me, don't you think?
You know, I haven't killed anyone in such a long time, and because
you are all, well, let's face facts, not very bright, I've decided to start off
my new fun by killing one of you!
Perhaps that will give you some focus this time.
And here's a little hint.
Pay attention now:

It's a name that starts with 'T.'

And his last day on earth will be: tomorrow!

Good luck!

Your old friend,

CS.

If a bomb had gone off in the middle of the city, it could not have produced a bigger reaction than the discovery of this unexpected letter.

Chief Inspector Yamashita, without a second thought, woke up the whole of the Kamakura police world, including people several ranks above him in the middle of the night, and the moment he told them what it was about, he was instantly informed he had *carte blanche* to proceed as he saw fit.

An hour later, he arrived by squad car at the central police station with the letter in a sealed evidence bag. He went straight to his office and awaited the still half-asleep head of forensics and several other key staff whom he had shaken from their beds to join him for an impromptu meeting to bring them up to speed on what needed to be done. Across the large station building, every light was now ablaze, and as the officers began to stumble in from across the city, the building began to buzz with anticipation that something really big had happened.

Yamashita's right-hand man, Detective Sergeant Yokota, knocked on his door shortly afterward, bearing coffee and more bad news.

"We traced the call made to your residence, sir. It was made from a burner phone, and we are still trying to establish the vicinity, but it's pretty broad."

Yamashita nodded. He had changed into his usual dark suit and tie, and was sitting at his startlingly tidy desk waiting for the files to be brought up from the records division.

"Right, well, that makes sense," he sighed. "The last time he did the exact same kind of thing, always used public phones, always hand-delivered letters and we never found a single print on anything. Not a hair. So, no reason for him to change now. This one is careful, Yokota. Very careful."

The younger officer leaned against the door frame. He was a heavy-set man with cropped hair, a serious manner and, in his spare time, a fifth-dan kendoist. He was also the best detective sergeant Yamashita had ever had.

"Sir, if you don't mind, a lot of this is way before my time. I wasn't even in the police force eighteen years ago. But I gather this is a pretty famous case, and there's been a lot of books and other stuff written about it? How do we know this is not some copycat or something?"

Yamashita smiled grimly and tapped his pen on the desk.

"We don't. Not officially. But I was on this case way back then, and I know this guy. I was a DS back then, like you. It's him, I'll stake my pension on it."

Yokota raised his eyebrows. In the three years he had been Yamashita's DS, he had never seen his usually imperturbable boss so agitated nor heard him make so many demands.

Another officer, a young woman, poked her head around the door.

"Sir, where do you want the files? There are…. a lot…" she said.

Yamashita nodded. "Well, there would be, I guess. We are going to need an incident room. Use the one on the second floor, I think traffic is doing something or other in there. Kick them out, clear the room. Get whiteboards, pens, all the usual stuff. I need it set up by 9 a.m. Clear?"

"Yes sir," the officer responded, and headed back to the records department to tell them where to take the more than fifty boxes of files that comprised the records on the original case that were still kept at the Kamakura station.

Yamashita turned to his DS again.

"Get everyone in here for the meeting, Yokota. Everyone. 9 a.m. No excuses. Understand?"

Yokota nodded and headed back to his desk to make some phone calls as soon as it was light. Unlike his boss, if he started calling people at 3 a.m., he would never hear the end of it.

Yamashita also bided his time now. It was too late to do anything other than send the necessary emails to people and wait for a more civilized time to get the ball rolling.

There were two people, however, whom he wanted to contact as soon as it was feasibly possible, so he waited until 5 a.m., and then he made his calls.

The first was to his old boss, the now-retired Chief Inspector Toyozaki, who had been in charge of the case when it had first started eighteen years before. His help was going to be indispensable now, and he knew it.

He dialed the number. He knew Toyozaki always went for a long walk in the early morning around where he lived, so he figured he was probably up and around and that he might be able to catch him before he left.

The phone rang for some time, and the familiar voice was finally on the other end.

"Toyozaki."

"Sir, it's Yamashita."

There was a brief pause while the older man gathered himself.

"Eiji. Good to hear from you. It's 5 a.m. What's going on?"

"Are you sitting down, sir?"

"I am, actually. Why?"

Yamashita tried to control himself, but it was little use. He knew exactly what this meant to both of them and many others in the force who had devoted years to the case.

"We have another letter. From CS."

This time there was dead silence for several seconds.

"You're sure of this?"

Yamashita could hear the barely controlled emotion behind his voice.

"Waiting on forensics, and I need to access the old files, of course. But yes, sir, I am. The letter is identical."

"Oh my God. OK. When did you receive it?"

"About five hours ago."

"Have you scheduled a meeting?"

"Yes sir. 9 a.m."

"I'll be there…. And Eiji…"

"Yes sir?"

"…Thank you."

Yamashita smiled. He had been worried recently about how the old fellow had been adjusting to retirement, and he knew this new information would make his day.

"No problem, sir. See you at nine."

Yamashita put down the receiver and sat back in his chair. This was not the time to be the bull in the china shop. He needed to proceed slowly, one step at a time. There could be no mistakes now. The letter had been right in that respect, this was indeed a second chance. God knew when they were going to get another.

The next call he knew he could make any time, but sooner was better than later, and she deserved to know about any developments in this case at once.

He dialed the number and waited. As expected, her old aunt answered the phone, but she was an early riser, and Yamashita knew it.

"Auntie Chen. Sorry for the early call. Can I speak to Fei-san?"

A few seconds later, Fei Chen was on the phone.

"Do you know what time it is?" came the familiar arched voice.

"I do," said Yamashita. "And I apologize, Fei-san. Can you come in for a meeting at 9 a.m.? I've asked everyone in, I'm afraid."

There was a slight pause on the other end as Fei processed the request.

"Of course. Eiji-san, what's this about?"

He and Fei were very old friends, and even without the early morning call, she could tell at once that something major had happened. Also, Fei was a coroner, and thus not under Yamashita's command at all, so it was a most unusual request from the senior detective.

"Well. I wanted you to hear it from me, that was all," said Yamashita slowly. "Fei... we have another letter from CS."

The was complete silence on the other end for several seconds, and Yamashita knew why.

"I'll be there. Thanks for letting me know."

The line went dead.

Yamashita replaced the receiver and leaned back in his chair. He took a long swig of the coffee Yokota had brought him and thought about Fei and how she had lost one of her best friends to this killer all those years ago.

If there was anyone who deserved to know about this, it was her.

======================

The incident room on the second floor was filled to overflowing at 9 a.m. when the chief inspector squeezed his way to the front and plugged in his laptop to the conference equipment. The room was full of uniformed officers, detectives, and forensic staff, as well as a scattering of senior officers and others joining online via video link from Tokyo and other places. His old boss, Chief Inspector Toyozaki, was also sitting at the front, and was being warmly greeted by many of his old colleagues who had rushed to meet him again.

Yamashita raised his hands for quiet. He tapped on his computer, and the big screen behind him lit up with a large picture of the letter, which caused an almost dead silence to descend on those gathered.

"Ladies and gentlemen," he began. "Just after midnight last night, a letter was delivered to my house from the killer who identifies himself as 'Climbing Silver'. I'm sure many of your more senior colleagues will know well enough to whom I am referring."

He paused for a moment to let his words sink in, and to watch the shock of understanding as it raced across the faces of many in the room.

"I know many of you were not even officers when this case first began, and we have not heard a word from this killer for the last eighteen years. Not since his last murder. So let me bring you up to speed a little, and I urge all of you who are not familiar with the case to immediately acquaint yourself with the details, which I will not go over in their entirety at this point. This case has never been closed, and his four victims to date await justice." He paused again momentarily and cleared his throat. "As far as we know, this letter is genuine. Let me now turn over to Chief Inspector Toyozaki, who was the officer in charge when all of this occurred. Sir?"

Toyozaki stood and faced the room, a tall, silver-haired man with a military bearing and the sort of face that told you at once that he brooked no nonsense. He wore an old tweed coat, a kind of signature for him, and his voice was deep and commanding, the kind of voice that when he spoke, you listened.

"Ladies and gentlemen, I wish I could say it is good to be back… maybe it is, in a way, if we can finally catch this person. This will be up to you, though," he paused and looked around the room.

"Chief Inspector Yamashita and I worked this case many years ago, a case which saw the death of four people, including one of our own officers. He has not and will not be forgotten, and we will get justice for him and the others. This I promise you."

He turned to the screen and picked up a laser pointer on the desk.

"This, ladies and gentlemen, is a letter from someone now popularly known in the media as the *Shogi* Ripper. Even those of you who were not here at the time may have heard the name, as there have been several books and many television shows and articles about this person, who committed some of the worst crimes this city has ever witnessed."

"This was received just a few hours ago. It has several features only the police know about, and thus we believe it to be genuine."

He raised the pointer to the screen and ran the bright red dot along the lines of script that were written vertically in Japanese characters.

"First of all, as should be obvious, the letter was written with a brush. It is by someone with a rather eclectic, almost artistic way of writing, and several calligraphic characteristics are pretty unique. Note the odd brushstrokes here, and here," he waved the pointer over several characters. "And also the signature 'CS', written in the roman alphabet as you can see, which is also quite a unique feature. The previous letters have never been disclosed to the press, so this is another pointer that the letter is indeed from this person. This brushwork has always been seen as a key identifier in the past."

"The letter is also in the same tone and length as the previous letters, and as you can see, it has this red seal at the bottom. This seal is identical to the previous letters, and again, has never been shown to the press."

He turned to face them with the utmost seriousness and paused again.

"Ladies and gentlemen, if this letter is real, and we believe it is, then someone else is going to die today. This person is a police officer, and the name apparently begins with 'T.' We have already contacted every such officer on our books and made them aware of this threat. Unfortunately, there are far too many of them to be protected properly by uniformed officers, and no doubt quite a number of you are in this room. Will you raise your hands, please?"

Several hands went up.

"OK, everyone, please take note of these people. I am among them myself. And those who raised your hands, please take extra precautions if you are alone anytime in the next twenty-four hours."

"This is not the end of this threat, however. The person who identifies himself as 'Climbing Silver' has killed at least four people that we know of. He has sent a letter like this before each of these killings, sometimes identifying the person by his initials, and sometimes giving the day the killing was to take place." He paused and looked around the room. "Now… pay attention to what I am about to say. He has *never* failed to make good on his threats. He has also *never* left behind a single clue, nor do we have any idea who this person is."

"This, my friends, must change."

He nodded at Yamashita, and took his seat again.

Yamashita looked out over the assembled officers, and saw Fei standing at the back of the room, her face ashen and frowning.

"Please pay attention to the following slides. The people whose pictures I am about to show you are the killer's previous victims. And all of the victims had some relationship to the game of *shogi*."

The screen changed and showed a picture of a woman who looked to be in her thirties.

"The first victim, Akiko Terumoto, found battered to death in her house in 1994. Her husband, Akihisa, a noted *shogi* player, was convicted of her killing but later acquitted. He is still alive, and living in Tokyo now."

The screen changed to another slide of two people, a man and a woman in their thirties.

"Police Constable Yasuo Enamoto and his wife, Sachie. The husband was a member of the same *shogi* club as Terumoto and lived next door to them. Both were found battered to death after Terumoto's conviction in 1995."

The screen changed once again, this time showing a man in his fifties.

"Watanabe Eikichi. A seventh *dan shogi* expert and head of the Watanabe *Shogi* School in Kamakura. Again battered to death at his home a few months later."

He looked up at Fei, white-faced and staring.

The screen changed again to show a large image of a *shogi* piece, known as the *kinsho* or gold general.

"In all cases, this same *shogi* piece was left with all of the bodies, usually clasped in one of their hands. This fact *has* become known to the press due to the husband's trial, and led to the name of the '*Shogi* Ripper,' which you no doubt have heard of in the media. The preferred name of the killer, 'Climbing Silver,' was written in full on the first-ever letter we received, which came just before the killing of officer Enamoto and his wife. Since that time, all of his letters have been signed 'CS'. For those unfamiliar with *shogi,* the name 'Climbing Silver' refers to a well-known opening system popularised by the noted player Michiyoshi Yamada and known as 'Yamada's Climbing Silver.' No connection to the opening other than the name the killer chose has ever been established.

"We will meet back here tomorrow morning at the same time for an update. That is all for the moment."

Most of the people filed out of the room, leaving only a core of selected officers behind who would be in charge of different aspects of the investigation.

Yamashita walked over to where Toyozaki was sitting and crouched down in front of him.

"Can you stay and help with this, sir?" he asked, looking him in the eyes.

Toyozaki nodded. "Of course. Believe me, I wouldn't miss it for the world," he said, grim-faced.

Chapter 3

The *Shogi* Ripper

That afternoon, Penelope found Fei sitting in her living room in her usual old wicker chair, staring out over the vegetable garden. It was nothing unusual to find Fei in her house, as they were neighbors as well as best friends and both of them had an interest in tending the garden together.

Fei was smoking her usual antique Japanese pipe, but there was something about her that seemed more thoughtful than usual, and Penelope had known her long enough to sense when her friend was worried about something.

"Is something wrong?" she asked, sitting down next to her.

Fei nodded sadly. "You're not going to believe this…. Yamashita-san called me into the office this morning for a big meeting. Everyone was there, even old Toyozaki. I thought he had retired long ago, but they've brought him back."

"Toyozaki-san? Wasn't that Eiji's old boss?"

"The very same," she nodded.

"So, what was it all about?"

Fei paused and tapped out her pipe into an old metal cup she used as an ashtray.

"They got another letter. After eighteen years…. Another letter…" she said softly.

Penny looked at her, confused.

"Another letter from who?"

Fei looked up at her and Penelope detected a note of anger in her voice.

"From the Ripper. From 'Climbing Silver.'"

Penelope sat back in her chair in shock.

"I'm so sorry, Fei," she said.

Fei nodded and refilled her pipe.

Penelope stared at her, worried. When Fei had been a young girl, she had been a member of the Watanabe School, a famous *shogi* school in Kamakura led by Eikichi Watanabe, one of the greatest *shogi* players of his generation. He had not only been her teacher, but almost like a second father as she had been growing up, and she had been welcomed into the family, where Watanabe had treated her like his own daughter.

They had remained close friends even as Fei had decided to follow a career in medicine rather than turn professional, and they had often met at *shogi* events and other social occasions, with the older professional making a point of attending Fei's more important tournaments to lend encouragement to his former protégé.

When he became the *Shogi* Ripper's fourth and final victim, Fei had been completely devastated by his loss, almost like she had lost her real father. It had taken her a long time to return to any semblance of normality, and it was only through Yamashita's persistence that she had also begun to play *shogi* again with anything like the same passion she had in the past.

"Do you want to talk about it?" asked Penelope.

Fei sighed.

"There's not much to say. They've got this new letter. I saw it, and they're right, it looks identical to the old ones. He is threatening to kill someone else, of course. And he probably will. There never seems much they can do to stop the maniac."

Penelope nodded. The last manhunt for the killer had lasted years, and the police must have interviewed half of the city of Kamakura. Even Penelope had been interviewed as she had also known the victim through Fei.

The case had, since the first murder, been seen as a simple murder of a wife by her husband, and the man had been convicted. However, he had been quickly acquitted by the Court of Appeal, in large part because the killings had continued after he was put in jail, but also because the prosecution's case against him had always been weak and circumstantial and his conviction had been seen by many as a gross miscarriage of justice. Chief Inspector Toyozaki had been held responsible when the acquittal had been announced, as the police had always been convinced that they had got their man. Toyozaki had been forced into retirement shortly afterward.

"Is there anything I can do?"

Fei stared out over the garden.

"Do you remember that journalist, I think his name was Nakamura? The one who wrote the book about the case?"

Penelope nodded. "Of course. He interviewed you. He was one of my old students."

"That's the one. You know, I'd like to talk to him again. There is something about Watanabe-*sensei's* death that's always bothered me. I just can't put my finger on it... but he might, I think. Anyway..."

Fei stood up.

"Let's water the plants. Those eggplants are about to keel over," she said with a half-smile.

Penelope got up and went with her into the garden. When Fei was like this, she knew it was best to try and give her something to do and to wait.

Later that evening, after Fei had left, Penelope went into her study and looked through her well-organized bookshelves for a book she had not read for several years. She found it straight away and took it over to her desk.

The Shogi Ripper was a popular book written by the investigative journalist Sal Nakamura, who had once been one of her students many years ago at Hassei university. He had been a talented writer even back then and had gone on to a career in journalism at some of Japan's leading newspapers. However, as a Kamakura native, he had been fascinated by the Ripper case to such a degree that he had spent several years investigating it. This book had been the result of his obsessive labors, and he had invited Penelope to the launch at his publisher's offices when it had come out. He had even interviewed Fei for the book due to her close relationship with the Ripper's last victim.

Sal had become convinced he knew who the ripper was, but his solution, no matter how carefully argued it had been, had been dismissed out of hand by the police, and nothing to her knowledge had been done about it since.

If anyone in the world had information that could help it, it was Sal, who possibly knew more about the case than the police. He really should know what was going on if he didn't already. Penelope decided to give him a call.

The phone rang for quite a long time, and Penelope had begun to wonder if she still had the right number. When he finally answered, he was delighted to hear from his old teacher, and also pleased that she was checking to know if he knew about the latest developments. When she informed him about the letter, he laughed out loud.

"Oh, Penny-*sensei*, yes, of course I know. The police department in Kamakura leaks like a sieve. Quite a shock, isn't it? After all these years too….."

"Yes, it certainly was. Are you still interested in the case? I mean, are you planning to write anything more about it?"

"Well, I wasn't up till today, but I may well do a second edition of the book if things develop. Why do you ask?"

"I was wondering if you would like to come over for dinner with Fei and I. There are a few things I would like to understand, particularly about the original case, and I also think it might do Fei good to talk about things as well. It's actually her suggestion. Do you think you would have the time?"

Nakamura said he would love to come, and they settled on a day later in the following week when Penelope hoped that Yamashita-san might be able to join them as well.

She hung up the phone and sat contemplating the cover of Sal's book in front of her on her desk. There was something about the case that had always struck a chord in her, particularly as someone who liked a challenge and hated loose ends, and there were quite a few things in the original case that she had always wondered about. Perhaps these intriguing inconsistencies were why it had drawn so much attention across Japan, especially if you agreed with Sal's ideas as to the fiendishly clever way the first murder may have been perpetrated.

Yamashita-san might also benefit from sitting down with a real expert on the case like Sal, someone who was not in the police force and where he could perhaps see things from a different perspective, so she decided to invite all of them to dinner. As usual, she was sure Fei would accuse her of doing too much, but Yamashita-san owed her a few favors, especially with the help she had given him in the Takahashi case the previous year, so she was fairly confident he would agree to come and meet Sal, even if just out of interest.

She tapped the cover of the book and said to herself, *"This time. This time we are going to get you....."*

=====================

It had been a gruelling day setting up the investigation, but on his departure from the Kamakura police station that evening, Yamashita had insisted that his old boss be accompanied home by a uniformed officer, someone who had been given explicit instructions about maintaining his safety that evening.

It was no coincidence that Yamashita was concerned for the older man, not only because of Toyozaki's close connection to the case, but also because of the simple fact that his name began with a 'T.' To him, that was more than enough cause to warrant increasing his security, despite the older officer's protestations that he could 'look after himself.'

He assigned a burly young police constable to take him home, a man he knew had spent several years in the defense forces and, more specifically, in the Special Forces Group, the Japanese version of the green berets.

As he left the building, the quiet young officer had saluted him smartly at the door of the squad car, and had driven Toyozaki home shortly before 10 p.m.

Toyozaki had greatly enjoyed his day back at the station, where he had been warmly greeted by his old colleagues and given a desk to work from in the incident room. It had been good to feel useful and to have his services valued once more by the police department to which he had given his whole working life. It especially felt good to be asked back to work on *this* case, which was the one responsible for the early termination of his career once the suspect had been acquitted, which had been a profound shock for everyone connected to the case and for the country as a whole. Yet no one had suffered more than Toyozaki, who had been the officer-in-charge and, therefore, the man who had to take the blame and fall on his sword for the good of the force.

Being given another chance to catch this criminal in one of the most famous cases in Japanese history was a dream come true for him in every way.

They arrived at his old home in about twenty minutes, which was located not far from the popular Hase temple, one of the city's most famous landmarks and a short drive from the city center.

They pulled into the quiet little street of old wooden houses where he lived, and the young officer got out of the car first and led the way through the gate to the front door.

"Could you open the door, sir? And wait here for a moment?" he said politely.

Toyozaki nodded. "Of course, be my guest. Don't mind the mess in the kitchen, I haven't had a chance to clean up yet…" he smiled.

He opened the door, and Toyozaki noted that the officer had his hand on his gun holster as he disappeared inside to check the house. The man was gone for perhaps a minute, and finally, he reappeared and nodded to him.

"Looks fine from what I can see, sir. Do you want me to stick around for a while?"

"No, not at all. I'm fine. I'll see you tomorrow at the station. Thanks for the lift." he said.

The officer saluted him crisply and left without another word.

Toyozaki waved him goodbye and went inside. He noted that the car did not move off immediately though, and guessed the young man would hang around for a while out of an abundance of caution. He couldn't blame him, he had been exactly the same when he was a young officer.

Toyozaki closed the door behind him and switched on the lights as he moved through the small house where he now lived alone. His wife had died some years before of cancer, and he had become used to the bachelor life again, but not the quiet of coming home to an empty house. Their only child, a son, had followed his father and grandfather's footsteps and was in the police force in western Tokyo these days. He had a family of his own now and rarely made it to Kamakura to see him, but it was something that he understood well, as he knew well the demands that were made of young officers, particularly in the capital. They talked on the phone once a week though, and for this contact he was grateful.

He went into the small living room which held the family altar, and gave the picture of his wife a nod of greeting.

"I'm home. It's been a long day," he told her. He often talked to her in the quiet of his days now, sometimes for hours. He chatted to her about what he had done that day, or whatever was happening in the world or on the news. He sometimes thought he talked more to her now than when she was alive.

He went into the kitchen, threw his coat over the back of a chair, and just as he had always done whenever he came home in the old days, took a bottle of beer out of the refrigerator as his reward. He sat down at the table, poured himself a glass, and put on the television, where he found the news was finishing on TBS.

He downed the glass of beer in a few gulps and sat back and smiled, satisfied with his day's work. Work was something he accepted, but if there was one thing he didn't really understand, it was retirement. Once he was in his fifties, he knew it was around the corner, yet somehow it had always been something that didn't apply to him. It was as if all the other people were one day going to stop getting up in the morning and going to work, but not him. In his mind, he was going to keep going and going, always moving on to the next case and the one after that.

He realized now that he had been living in a state of denial, and when retirement had finally come, the forced inactivity and lack of purpose had completely blindsided him.

Suddenly, overnight, he had absolutely nothing to do. He was no longer a police officer, he had no duty to anyone or anything - it was just over. It was a complete mystery, like he had suddenly woken up in another country where he didn't know a soul. The job, he realized, had totally consumed his every waking moment. His whole identity was constructed around being Chief Inspector Toyozaki, the man in charge, the one everyone else looked up to and depended on.

It had taken him months to realize it, but he finally understood that he had not even done the most basic planning for retirement. He had no interests other than work, no hobbies, and no idea whatsoever what to do with the seemingly endless hours between getting up in the morning and going to bed.

But now, at least, his constant, nagging boredom, something he had never learned to live with and that followed him around like the proverbial black dog, had been lifted for what was going to be a brief respite, he knew. But it was still a respite, and he was more grateful for it than he could say.

Sitting there that night, having a glass of beer after a long day at the office, he felt a sense of pride, a resurgence of self-worth, and yes, a feeling of sheer happiness that had been absent for many years.

He reached for the remote control to turn up the sound, and that was when he sensed, for the first time, that he was not alone.

Someone was standing behind him.

This feeling may have been the last thing that Chief Inspector Toyozaki ever knew, and no one would ever know if he had time to act or even time to think or call out.

When Toyozaki failed to arrive at the station the next morning, Yamashita immediately sensed something was not right. The older man was a stickler for punctuality and had never had a day off in his life. He certainly was not going to start now, Yamashita reasoned. He had called and received no answer, and had immediately sent two uniformed officers to the house, where they had found the front door unlocked.

Yamashita had been in his car less than a minute later, racing to the scene with the siren screaming in the morning traffic.

The body was slumped against the kitchen cabinets, and blood spatter covered the floors and walls around the little room. The autopsy, which had later been conducted by Fei, revealed that the victim's head had been caved in with repeated blows from a hammer-like weapon, and his death, mercifully, had been quick, if not instantaneous.

Hours later, as he stood amongst the blood and carnage of this decent man's end, all he could feel was a sickening sense of rage. The forensic crew was still at work, and a large group of officers had cut off the entire street and were interviewing the neighbors.

The television was still on, and Yamashita asked the forensics people if he could turn it off. The silence in the little room when he had done this, was deafening.

Yamashita had been expecting one more detail, and sure enough, it was there.

In the victim's right hand, turned palm up and resting on the floor, was a *shogi* piece: the gold general, the *kinsho*.

It was later surmised that the killer might have been hiding in one of the large bedroom cupboards, perhaps covered in some blankets and *futon* that were stored there, but this explanation, however likely, was impossible to confirm, and no significant DNA or clothing fibers had been found. The door to the house had not been forced, but there were some tool marks on one of the rear windows, which had not been fitted with a grill, and it was assumed that this was the most likely way the killer had got inside.

As always with this killer, there was no DNA, no fingerprints, and no clue of any kind for them to find.

A tear rolled down his cheek, and he quickly brushed it away before the technician taking fingerprints from a fallen beer bottle on the floor could see.

Chapter 4

First Blood

The first few weeks after the death of Chief Inspector Toyozaki went by in a blaze of activity for his former protégé. However, as things stood and, much to their disappointment, they made no progress whatsoever. No clues had been left at the scene of the crime, and there were no cameras in any of the streets around the home that showed anything even remotely like someone acting suspiciously. They had also drawn a total blank with the neighbors, who had neither seen nor heard a single thing. The former chief inspector had been an intensely private individual, and many of his closest neighbors neither spoke to him nor were even aware he had been in the police force.

A detailed forensic report on the letter and its envelope had also revealed nothing. It was written on the same commonly available paper as the previous letters of eighteen years prior, with a fine-tipped brush as was widely used everywhere, and with the same kind of ink used by every school child in Japan when they learned *shuji* or Japanese calligraphy. Three graphologists had also confirmed the writing as being from the same person who had written the previous letters, a fact that Yamashita had already been fully convinced of right from the first moment he had laid eyes on it.

In short, the whole investigation had ground to a complete halt, and they were no further advanced than they had been eighteen years before when the last body had been discovered.

Given this miserable state of affairs, Yamashita, who had slept several nights recently on the couch in his office and eaten nothing but what was available at the closest convenience store to the station, decided that he might as well take the night off and happily accepted the chance of a home-cooked meal at Penelope's house. Besides the offer of hot food, he was also interested in discussing the case with Sal Nakamura, whose journalistic work he respected and whom he had been informed would be there too.

When he arrived at the old house, he found Penelope, Fei and Sal already halfway through their first bottle of chablis and the delicious smell of Penelope's beef stroganoff drifting through the house.

He was warmly greeted and shook hands with Sal, whom he had not seen for some years since he had provided him with some off-the-record interviews for his book. Yamashita, unlike many in the rather close-minded and insular world of Japanese law enforcement, was happy to seek out the opinions of others, even journalists and criminals, if it would help shed light on a case, and also maintained a wide circle of highly accomplished and intellectual friends in his personal life. Sal, he regarded as one of these.

Penelope, who had also not seen Sal in some years, found him refreshingly unchanged. He was a tall, lanky man in his mid-forties now, with the same long ponytail he had sported in his days as a student at Hassei, albeit now it was marked with long streaks of grey, as was his goatee, which had also never changed. His real name was Koichi, but he preferred to go by the nickname of Sal, after J.D. Salinger, who had been his favorite author in high school. He also still wore the same thick, black-framed glasses, and in his hand there was the ever-present hand-rolled cigarette made from pungent *Drum* tobacco.

"Would you like some chablis?" Penelope said as she topped up everyone's glasses.

"Absolutely," said Yamashita, easing himself into one of the dining table chairs. "I think I've earned it."

"That you have, I'm sure," said Fei, who was smoking her usual old pipe with one of Penelope's cats on her lap. "Any news?"

Yamashita shook his head and removed his necktie.

"Nothing, not a thing," he said with a shrug. "I guess you already know that, though," he said to Sal, who nodded and gave him a consoling smile. Yamashita was well aware that good investigative journalists of Sal's standing had deep relationships with all levels of the police force and government, especially young and impressionable junior officers who thought being taken for a drink by a well-known author like Sal was a bit of a thrill.

"Yeah," said the journalist as he rolled another cigarette. "I heard that you guys had come up empty. I'm not really surprised, though. It seems of a pattern with the old killings." He lit his cigarette with his old Zippo lighter and leaned forward.

"By the way, I'm sorry to hear about old Toyozaki. I knew you guys were close."

Yamashita nodded sadly.

"Yeah, that's true. I learned just about everything I know about policing from him. The man was a meticulous investigator, whatever other faults he may have had."

"That's true," said Fei, who had also known him. "He was one of the good guys. I never thought I would find him on the table in front of me." She looked away at the darkened windows, and Penelope's heart went out to her. It seemed like she had lost too many old friends recently.

She served the food, and they talked about other matters for a while, especially Nakamura's purchase of an old, deserted home in the mountains of Nagano, where the journalist was regularly staying these days.

"The place is old," he said. "I mean seriously old and really cold in the winter. It still has one of those wood-fired bathtubs like in the old days. You know, where you have to go outside and get the fire going in a little box outside the bathroom and stuff. Everybody told me to get rid of it, like my sister who absolutely hated it when she visited, but I dunno, I kind of like it. Chopping firewood is kind of cathartic, I find."

Yamashita laughed. "Maybe I should try it. I need something cathartic these days."

Penelope served them a tiramisu for dessert, which she knew Fei and Yamashita liked.

"I have a question, folks," said Penelope, interrupting them. "Can anybody tell me the details about why the first suspect, what was his name, Terumoto? Why was he acquitted, and is he still around?"

Sal glanced at Yamashita, as if to ask for permission.

"Go ahead Sal, you know as much about it as me," he said with a wave of his fork.

Sal nodded, pushed his plate away and lit up another cigarette.

"Yeah, Penny-*sensei*. That's what makes this whole case so special. Somebody once described it as like the champagne of murder mysteries. Honest, you won't find a better one. Are you ready? Let me tell you a story then…."

"Akihisa Terumoto. He was about fifty years old or so back then and one of the best *shogi* players in the country. Had his own school he'd inherited from his dad, Morio, who came from a long line of top *shogi* players stretching back over one hundred and fifty years. His preferred opening when he was an active pro? Yes, you guessed it. 'Yamada's Climbing Silver.' He was one of the leading experts on the opening. He'd even written one of the standard textbooks on it."

Fei nodded. "Yes, I have it. I studied it a lot as a girl."

"Me too. I have a signed copy of it at home as well," said Yamashita.

"OK," said Sal. "I see you guys are fans. Anyway, let's talk about what happened that night."

He took a swig of wine and cleared his throat.

"So Terumoto goes to play at a certain *shogi* club in Kamakura, where there are a lot of advanced players."

"Yes," said Fei. "I used to go there too when I was a kid. An old place near the station, isn't it?"

"That's the one," said Sal. "Terumoto leaves his wife, Akiko, at home and sets off to play. Tonight before he arrives, though, there is a telephone call. The caller, a

44

woman, asks if someone could give Terumoto a message. Sure, the guy answering says. And this guy is an ex-judge, by the way, and sort of the club captain there."

"Please tell Terumoto to come to this address tonight at 7 p.m. to discuss a business proposal." He gives the captain an address in eastern Kamakura, near Yuigahama beach. "Tell him it's very important, and my boss must speak to him urgently. The name is Kuramoto. It's very urgent and in his interest. Please don't forget." And she hangs up. So the captain writes it all down, and when Terumoto appears, he gives him the information. Apparently, this guy Kuramoto is a well-known *shogi* publisher, and Terumoto and some others know the name."

"OK," said Penelope. "So far, so good."

Sal smiled. "Right then. Here's where it gets interesting. So pay attention. Terumoto turns around because he thinks it is important and sets off for the house of the mysterious Kuramoto. He takes the bus from Kamakura station and makes a point of telling the driver to shout out when they arrive at the stop at Yuigahama beach. The driver remembers this because Terumoto makes a big deal of it and reminds him twice. So when they get there, Terumoto gets off and thanks him kindly. If something strikes you as odd about this, you would be spot on, because Terumoto is a Kamakura native born and bred, and everyone knows where Yuigahama beach is, right?"

Heads nodded all around the table.

"Terumoto wanders off down the road, but now he can't find the house. Or so he says. He asks at the local convenience store. Does anybody know this address? They tell him they don't. He asks them if they know the time.

They tell him it's nearly 7 p.m. He keeps walking around, looking. It's after 7 p.m. now. He goes into two different shops, a *sake* shop, and a little fruit and vegetable shop, both run by locals who know the area backwards. They both tell him they have never heard of it. He asks them the time too. It's like getting on to 7.30 p.m. now. So he gives up. He returns to the bus stop and goes home the same way."

"Now," said Sal, leaning forward and rubbing his hands together. "When he gets home, he knocks on his neighbor's door. That's police constable Enamoto and his wife, Sachie. whom Terumoto knows quite well. Enamoto is also a *shogi* player and plays at the police club. I think that's the same one you guys play at, right?"

Fei and your Yamashita nodded. "The very same. We both knew him," said Fei. "He was a nice guy."

"Anyway," Sal continued. "He tells his neighbor he's lost his key. Enamoto has a spare, as Terumoto does to his place, as they have this standing arrangement to look after one another's cats when one of them is on holiday."

"Terumoto tells them he's knocked and called, but his wife seems to be out. Enamoto and his wife are both at home, so they come next door with Terumoto with the key and open the door for him. And that's when he finds his wife's body in the living room. She's on the floor with her head caved in, and there is blood everywhere. And, of course, on her body is the *shogi* piece, the gold general."

Sal finished his wine. "And that's how the whole thing kicks off."

Penelope poured him another glass.

"OK, but why did the police think he was so guilty?"

Yamashita smiled. "I assume that question is directed to me. Give me a beer, and I'll tell you."

"Deal," said Fei, going to the refrigerator and placing a can of beer and a glass on the table in front of him.

"Well," he began. "We always tend to start with the husband whenever a wife is killed. Ninety percent of the time, we are right too."

"Another reason not to get married," said Penelope, looking at Fei, who nodded vehemently.

"That being said, Terumoto gave us no reason to look elsewhere, either. His behavior was suspicious from the start. And the whole thing, the way he had behaved that night, looked like classic alibi-building. Toyozaki and I were convinced of it. For example, the phone call to the *shogi* club, let's start there. He could have made an accomplice do it. Or just tricked someone into calling, saying it was a prank or something."

"Then all this stuff with the bus driver. Asking him twice to remember the stop. Checking the time, making a big deal of it. All so the guy remembers him, of course. Then the same thing at the three shops. Three! Like he's going out of his way to make those people remember him too. He keeps asking them the time. Of course, there's no such address, and there's no such Kuramoto. The real Kuramoto, who is indeed a *shogi* publisher, lives in Tokyo and has never contacted Terumoto in his life."

"Still no evidence he did it, though," said Penelope. "The real killer could have set him up to get him out of the house while he killed the wife."

Yamashita finished his beer and banged down the glass on the table for emphasis.

"Exactly," he said. "Exactly what got him off too...but...."
he leaned forward and looked at them one by one.

"There was the woman thing," interjected Sal.

Yamashita wagged his finger at him.

"Yes, the woman thing. It seems Terumoto and his wife
both had secrets they kept from each other."

"Yep, very true," said Sal. "He was quite the ladies' man
and had relationships with several of his female students in
the past. I was pretty convinced that Akiko, the wife, knew
about it too. As wives often do. Anyway, Akiko is like ten
years younger than him, quite good-looking, and she's been
serving him a dish of cold revenge with the local insurance
guy and one of Terumoto's older students for some time, a
guy called Taniyama."

Yamashita nodded. "Also a notorious ladies' man, but he
appeared genuinely distraught at what had happened to his
girlfriend, plus he had an alibi. A good one, too, unlike
Terumoto."

"Wow. Quite a lot of dirt and mystery already," said
Penelope.

"Yes," said Yamashita. "As Sal said, this is the champagne
of murder mysteries. Anyway, once we find out about all his
women, Toyozaki is convinced that's motive. Kill the wife,
take off with the latest mistress. And so he arrests him. We
reviewed his so-called alibi meticulously, and there were
enough gaps for him to have done it. The coroner at the
time, you remember your old boss, Dr. Shimada, right Fei?
He puts the time of death at around 5:00 p.m., which means
he did have time to kill her before he went out."

Fei snorted. "Yes, I remember him well—the laziest
coroner in Japan. As I recall, he had no real evidence to say

that time. He didn't even do a proper rectal exam to measure the body temperature. He just guessed it, and wrote 5 p.m. on the report. Typical of him, I always thought," she said and rolled her eyes.

"Yes, and it was a crucial mistake that blew up in our faces at the acquittal procedure. But at the original trial, Terumoto's lawyer never questioned it. That wasn't the case at the acquittal though, when they showed that given the way old Shimada had done the autopsy that we had no real case for saying the time of death was 5pm. It could have been much later, meaning Terumoto was possibly in the clear. Still, at the time, Toyozaki is still convinced, even though all the evidence is totally circumstantial. As far as we were concerned, he was as guilty as sin".

"What about the murder weapon?" asked Penelope.

"Never found," said Sal. "Nor was there a drop of blood on him or his clothes because Enamoto stopped him from touching the body when it was discovered, good cop that he was. Toyozaki maintained he still would have had time to get changed, get rid of his clothes and the murder weapon, which was possible. We might have had better luck with the forensic testing we can do today, but that was back then... so...."

"And so," continued Yamashita, "he was tried and convicted. But there was a huge public outcry. No evidence, no weapon. Then the Justice Minister got involved because he was looking for votes, presumably. And there was another trial, and he was acquitted. But, of course, the thing which really crucified us was that there were three more absolutely identical killings while he was in jail. First, the Enamotos, the neighbors. Both were killed the same way.

Both left with the same *shogi* piece in their hands. Then… Watanabe," he looked at Fei, who nodded silently.

"And that was that. He was free," said Sal.

There was silence around the table for a while.

"So the Enamoto couple… why were they killed, do you think?" asked Penelope.

Sal shrugged. "The only reason I can think of is that Enamoto was a *shogi* player. That seems to be the common thread."

"Did his wife play *shogi*?"

"I don't think so. She wasn't a member of any club I know," he said.

"Terumoto's wife didn't play *shogi* either, did she?"

"No. She had no interest in the game," replied Yamashita.

"And Toyozaki-san?"

Nakamura and Yamashita looked at each other.

"No, he didn't play, as far as I know."

"Hmmm… It would seem then that not *all* the victims were *shogi* players then. They were somehow connected… to the case. The case against Terumoto. Would that be a fair assumption?" she asked.

Yamashita raised his eyebrows.

"Yes. That would be fair. So… what are you driving at?"

Penny raised her wine glass and swirled the contents meditatively.

"You know, I'm not sure," she said. "There is just something wrong about this whole thing. I don't understand it, the motive, I mean. If you want to kill *shogi* players, why choose Enamoto? Enamoto was a player, that's true, but he was connected to the case against

Terumoto, right? As was his wife. So my point is, why kill *them*? Why not kill another *shogi* player?" Penelope pondered.

"He did," said Fei. "He killed Watanabe."

Penelope nodded. "And Watanabe-*sensei* had no connection to Terumoto?"

Yamashita folded his arms and smiled. "None at all. Zero. They never even played each other. We checked."

"I see. Well, maybe that's the connection."

"Sorry?" said Fei.

"Maybe the connection is…. that they didn't have a connection," said Penelope.

Fei laughed out loud.

"Sorry, folks. Too much chablis, I think."

Sal also laughed and jokingly topped up Penelope's glass.

"Would you like to see him, Penny-*sensei*?" he asked.

Penny looked up. "Who?"

"Terumoto,"

Penny leaned forward. "He's still around?"

Sal nodded. "Still around. Still playing *shogi*. Likes to keep a low profile these days. How about next week?"

Penelope nodded. "Yes, please. I would. That would be very interesting."

Sal smiled. "OK, no problem. I'll set it up."

Penelope clapped her hands excitedly.

Yamashita was quiet and regarded Penelope calmly, considering what she said.

"You should be careful, Penny. I still haven't given up on Terumoto. I still consider him dangerous."

"Don't worry, I have Sal here to look after me," she smiled.

Sal leaned in towards the table.

"I agree with Yamashita-san, actually. As you probably know. I think he did it too. But that opinion is not very popular down at police headquarters these days, is it?"

Yamashita smiled his gentle smile. "No, you're right. But I'm not in this for the popularity... more wine, anyone?"

Chapter 5

The Girl in the Painting.

Ginza is one of the most famous shopping districts in the world, and by far the most famous in Japan. Despite the average Japanese housewife being renowned for their devotion to parsimony, the whole area was devoted to a love of high-quality goods and services and the prices that went with them. Anything bought here tended to be on a level of extortion usually only found in the company of hardened criminals, whether it was a melon that cost as much as a designer handbag or a designer handbag that cost a similar amount to a new car.

No one minded. It was, after all, Ginza.

Located right in the heart of Tokyo and containing the marvellous old *kabuki-za* theatre, the home of the *kabuki* stage play in the capital and not far from the Imperial Palace and the iconic Tokyo station, the district has one of the biggest and most famous assortments of high-end department stores and brand shops in the country.

It was also a haven for the capital's art world.

There are dozens of small art galleries in Ginza, an old name that means 'silver mint,' as it was one of the first places in the country to produce coinage in the early seventeenth century. And it seemed that nearly every time Penelope was invited to an exhibition of one kind or another, which was frequently, it was held somewhere in Ginza, and autumn seemed the most popular time for these things.

A week after the moon-viewing party, she had received a postcard inviting her to an exhibition of Mari Setouchi's latest paintings, with a personal note written on the back telling her when and what time to come.

Exhibitions for famous painters like Mari were usually quite popular, and it was impossible just to drop in whenever you felt like it as you could at the myriad of other art galleries in Ginza featuring lesser-known names. As a result, it was invitation only, and if you wanted to go, you had to call the gallery in advance and make sure your name was on the appropriate list for that day and time.

Penelope had also received an invitation for Fei, and after a short discussion, where she managed to persuade her to come with the promise of going somewhere to eat *yakitori* later, art, which was never very high up Fei's list of essential interests, was added to their afternoon schedule.

When they arrived, they saw that the gallery, which was located just off Harumi street and not far from the famous Mitsukoshi department store, was quite a large exhibition space compared to many of Ginza's other usually much smaller galleries.

On entering, the first person they saw was Suwamoto-san, who they knew was a big fan of the artist. He made a beeline straight for them, dressed in a rather fashionable blue jacket and a cravat that matched the handkerchief in his pocket.

"So Penny-*sensei*, nice to see you! And Fei-san too. Are you here to look or to buy?" he asked teasingly.

Penelope put on a look of mock horror.

"I would say just look, especially at what I expect they charge in here. Are you buying more? Of course, you are. I can see it in your eyes…".

Suwamoto paused and stroked his chin.

"Well… I wasn't going to… but now I'm here, I don't know if I can resist. Some of these new paintings are quite something. Have a look around, why don't you, and you can give me your sage opinion."

"I'll do that. Have your credit card ready," she said, and nabbing two glasses of white wine from a passing waiter, she and Fei made their way around the gallery.

It wasn't long before they found what they were looking for.

"Wow. Look at that," said Fei pointing to an eye-catching painting that occupied the whole of the far wall. "That's the niece, isn't it?"

Penelope nodded. "Yes, definitely her," she said.

The large painting was clearly of Suzume. She was nude with her long hair loose against a bright green background, crouched down, and looking back over her shoulder right into the viewer's eyes. In the corner of the picture, and looking at her in a slightly quizzical way, was a beautifully detailed golden bird with a long black speckled tail which seemed about to speak to her. In the grass in front of her was an empty *shogi* board surrounded by autumn leaves, and between the fingers of her outstretched right hand she held a *shogi* piece in the classical way all players did, between the index and middle fingers, but it seemed like she had completely forgotten it was there, like you had distracted somehow in the act of placing it on the board. The picture had a dreamlike quality about it, and the juxtaposition of the bird and the young girl was both striking and, at the same time, quietly sensual.

"Wow, that is something," said Fei.

"Yes, it is…it's so… I don't know, loving in a way. The bird is almost kind of … maternal…" agreed Penelope.

"I'm glad you like it… I didn't realize you knew so much about art, Penny-*sensei*." said a voice behind them.

They both turned, and standing behind them was the artist herself, holding a glass of wine like them.

"Thank you both for coming. I was hoping I could see you again…" said Mari.

Penelope smiled. "It's a lovely exhibition," she said.

"Well, it's been quite a lot of work to put it together. You don't know how many moving parts there are in a show like this. But it seems to be working out. So, you like my Suzume?"

"Yes, it's really striking. Was she a good model?"

"Actually, no. She was absolutely terrible. Getting that girl to hold still for more than five minutes is impossible. I ended up working off photographs in the main. But at least she didn't mind taking her clothes off. You'd be surprised how many people don't like to do that."

Penelope wasn't surprised at all, but kept that to herself.

"Considering you're her aunt, that was rather game of her, I think," said Fei. "Is she here? I was hoping I could say hello."

Mari turned and looked around the room.

"Well, I'm sure she was here a minute ago. Yes, there she is, over there in the corner."

At that moment, Suzume turned, caught their eye, and made her way over to them.

"This is a really beautiful picture of you. How lucky you are to have such a talented aunt," said Penelope.

Suzume blushed. "I'm glad you like it, but it's a bit embarrassing," she said, casting her aunt a dark look. I just keep hoping nobody recognizes me. If I could grow a beard, I swear to you I would. I couldn't ask any of my friends to come here, especially my *shogi* friends. I would die a thousand deaths if they did. But you're right, I like it actually," she smiled. "It's hard not to…."

"That's my girl," said Mari with a smile. "OK. I have to go mingle. I'll leave you to it. Please make sure you say goodbye before you go, OK?"

Mari left and went over to see some of the other guests, leaving Penny and Fei to be escorted around the gallery by Suzume, who seemed to know quite a lot about the other paintings.

After viewing what was on display, none of which was the equal of the portrait of her niece, which was clearly the centerpiece of the exhibition, Penelope turned to her.

"I was wondering Suzume-san, where do you study *shogi*? I hear you go to a school in Kamakura?"

Suzume smiled, obviously happier to discuss this particular topic than her painting.

"Well, that's the reason I came to Kamakura. I was raised in Akita, actually, and there is absolutely nothing up there as far as *shogi* schools go. Just snow and bears. But there is a very good school here, and I had heard a lot about the teachers there, so I wanted to train with the master. My teacher in Akita recommended me, and I was lucky enough to get in, so I've been training there for the last six months.

"So both your parents live in Akita?"

"Just my mother, I never knew my father. Aunt Mari used to visit a lot though, especially when I was young. So I've always known her well."

"So tell me, is this a famous school? I'm sorry, I don't know much about *shogi*, that's Fei's domain."

"Yes, it's reasonably well known, isn't it?" she said, turning to Fei, who nodded.

"You might be interested in this actually, Penny. We were talking about it at the moon viewing. It's the Okamoto school you are at, right?" she said.

Suzume nodded. "Yes, that's the one."

"Oh, really?" said Penelope. "I haven't heard of it."

"Actually, you have," said Fei. "It used to be the Terumoto school, wasn't it, Suzume?".

Suzume nodded. "Yes, there was some big problem many years ago, and the school merged with the Okamoto school. But I still study under Terumoto-*sensei*. He's the head trainer there. Okamoto-san is quite old, we don't see him that much."

Penelope's eyes widened. "Really?" she asked, surprised.

"Yes, but that's not the Terumoto you're thinking of, though," said Fei. "Not the one we were discussing the other night at dinner. This is Terumoto Yasuo, the son. The father left the school, after his er…. legal problems," she said obliquely.

"Yeah," said Suzume nodding. "I heard there were some issues there years ago with Yasuo-*sensei's* father. I don't

58

really know what it was all about, however. I did hear they don't speak. The school has a good reputation though, and they have produced quite a few professional players over the years. That's why I wanted to join."

"Oh, never mind, I was just wondering. So, you are thinking about becoming a professional?" she asked.

Suzume nodded seriously. "Yes. That's my dream. It's possible, but it's a pretty hard road. And maybe I'm a little too old. I don't know, but I think I have a chance."

"Oh, that's wonderful," said Penelope encouragingly.

"Actually," said Fei. "I think she has more than a chance. You're currently at the third *dan*, and for your age at that level, which is the same as mine by the way, and I'm a *lot* older than you, I think you have an excellent chance of joining the professional ranks. God knows we need to get more women involved in *shogi*."

"It's up to the next few tournaments," said Suzume. "If I can do well, I may be able to get in. But the competition is pretty stiff… Anyway, I'll do my best."

"We'll keep our fingers crossed for you."

They were just about to make their farewells when Suwamoto joined them again.

"So, what did you think? What should I do?"

Fei smiled at him and took him by the arm to stand in front of Suzume's portrait.

Suwamoto sighed. "Of course, of course, you know me well. That's exactly the piece I was thinking of. It's stunning, isn't it?"

"It really is," said Penelope joining them in front of the portrait. "But I assume the price is equally stunning. But that's the one I would recommend as well. Fei only likes it because it's got some *shogi* in it." she laughed.

"Each to his own," said Fei. "Anyway, we will leave you to decide. I hope I can see it on your wall next time we visit," she said.

Suwamoto smiled and nodded. "OK, you two ladies just cost me a lot of money. I'm going to go and negotiate with Mari-san."

"OK, we'll come with you, I want to say goodbye anyway."

They found Mari on the other side of the crowded gallery and made their farewells.

Mari drew Penelope aside for a moment.

"Would you like to come to dinner at my house sometime? There are a few things I would love to show you if you have the time. And Fei-san too, of course. She could maybe play some *shogi* with Suzume. She needs a bit of competition, and I haven't played for many years…."

Penelope said she would be delighted to come, and they left it to Mari to organize a date.

Later on, when they were taking the train back to Kamakura, Penelope was sitting engrossed in a novel when she felt Fei nudge her.

"Just wondered, did you notice the *shogi* piece that Suzume was holding in the painting?"

Penelope looked up at her. "I can't say I did, it was a bit obscured. Did you?"

Fei smiled. "I did. It was half-covered by her finger, but it was either the *kinsho* or the *ginsho*. The gold or the silver general. They look pretty similar. I just thought that was a coincidence, given what we talked about the other night."

"It is, isn't it? Mind you, there could be any reason for that, it's just a nod to Suzume's interests, I guess."

"Maybe so. But I was just looking around the internet. You know. For birds like that. What do you think of this?"

Fei held up her phone and showed her an image of another painting of a very similar bird to the one Mari had painted, only in Mari's picture, the tail was longer and more detailed.

"That does look like the same bird, doesn't it?" said Penelope.

"Yes, it does."

Fei scrolled down the page a little and showed her the title:

Golden Pheasant
Mark Gertler, 1932

"How about that? I wonder why she chose that bird," Fei asked. "By the way, have you been following the newspapers? There is a lot of talk about the *Shogi* Ripper again."

"Yes, it's all over the papers and TV. You can't miss it."

"Of course, they are all talking about the old killings and the Terumoto case and all that. I heard someone describing the Toyozaki killing as an act of revenge," said Fei.

"Revenge for what? They never caught the real killer."

"I think it's a bit of a dig at Terumoto. A lot of people still think he had something to do with it. His alibi was just so suspicious."

Penelope frowned. "I don't know. The man might be completely innocent. Despite what Sal and Yamashita-san think."

"I would say he was. After all, all those other killings took place after he was in jail. There's no doubt about it," said Fei

"That's true." Penny sat back in her seat and crossed her arms. "It would seem to rather draw a line under things as far as Terumoto was concerned, I think. But I *would* like to know a bit more about him. There has to be more to this than just *shogi* and randomness. There has to be something else at play here. Something *personal*. All those victims were carefully selected, related to *shogi,* or the case, or both. I think someone knows all these people somehow. What's got me really puzzled is why the killer has suddenly reappeared. Why come back when you have gotten away with it? Why kill a senior police officer? That seems to be just begging to get caught. Why take the risk?"

Fei agreed. "Yes, that does seem very odd. Oh, and by the way… don't forget, you promised me *yakitori*. And I'm starving…."

"Don't worry," said Penelope, patting her hand. "My word is my bond," she said.

Chapter 6

Sins of the Father

Sal Nakamura was also as good as his word, and about a week later, Penelope received a phone call from him.

The police were no further along in their investigation than before, and the public and the media were now making increasingly angry calls on them to do something about the situation. Every day in the press, the Terumoto case and the *Shogi* Ripper were discussed on the more important news programs and also the ubiquitously inane variety shows that populate every channel in Japan, where the 'expert' panels' enjoyed the buzz and the chance to rake up as much sensational detail as they possibly could. One show that Penelope had caught because Fei insisted on watching it had speculated that Terumoto's wife's lover may have carried out the killings, only naturally enough, there was not a shred of evidence to support such a claim, any more than there was to accuse Terumoto. It seemed every day that more and more crackpot conspiracy theories and other way-out ideas found a home in the media and particularly online, where a number of the existing '*Shogi* Ripper" sites and forums that had lain dormant for years had now seen new life breathed into them, much to their joy.

"Not to be a ghoul," said Sal, "but did you know my book is now back in the top ten in the country? Talk about something rising from the dead…" he said with a smile.

Penny laughed. "Well, at least that is one positive thing about all of this, then. It's always been a fairly popular book, I thought. I mean, I see it around and in bookshops," she said.

"Apparently, the publisher had to rush out a bunch more copies. They had totally run out."

"Well, I'm pleased to hear that. No one is running around reprinting any of my books on long-dead Edo Period poets, that's for sure. Maybe I should start writing about serial killers too… So, are you going to take me to see Mr. Terumoto?"

"Yes," said Sal. "That's exactly why I called. Are you still interested?"

"Absolutely," said Penelope. "Only I hope we are not going to be intruding on the poor man or anything."

"Hmmm… I dunno about the 'poor man' thing. I still think he knocked off his wife. But I guess he's entitled to his privacy. I think I can manage things so that he doesn't know we are there, though." said Sal, who had obviously done this before.

"OK then," said Penelope. "Let's do it. It sounds exciting. I'm very curious to see what he looks like after all these years."

"Well, he looks pretty different. I don't know if you'll even recognize him. Let's see though…."

Two evenings later, Sal picked her up in his old Toyota Harrier, a large black car with tinted windows and a Buddhist rosary swaying from the rear-vision mirror ("for luck," Sal explained.) Penny was dressed in jeans and an old sweater as instructed and looked like someone just popping out to the supermarket for some milk.

Due to a near total lack of parking anywhere nearer, Sal had parked at the end of Penelope's little street, and when she opened the car door, she wondered if anyone would be able to tell what he did for a living from the look of it. He seemed to have a lot of boxes and other things in the back, including several large camping items and various bits and pieces of camera equipment. If he had been some kind of avid bird watcher, she would not have been at all surprised.

"Sorry about the mess in here," Sal apologized as she put on her seatbelt. "I'm always dragging things to and from Nagano these days, and sometimes it just gets left here."

Penny smiled and told him not to worry. In all the years she had lived in Japan, and despite having a license, she had never driven anything other than the occasional rental car. She had everything she needed within walking or cycling distance of her old wooden house in Kamakura and often wondered at her neighbors, many of whom owned cars that never left their driveways from one week to the next.

They headed east in the direction of the little suburb of Ikegami in Tokyo's Ota ward and after about an hour's drive, pulled into a little side street not far from the train station.

"Well, this is exciting," said Penelope. "I never thought one of my students would be taking me on a stakeout," she joked.

Sal smiled. "Well, don't get too excited. Stakeouts are usually pretty boring. Fortunately for us, our friend Terumoto is a man of habit. You can just about set your clock by him."

He checked his watch just for emphasis.

"See that little house down the street on the left with the old black mailbox in front?"

Penny craned her neck and finally saw what Sal was indicating.

"That's his house. He's lived here ever since he left Kamakura after the acquittal. It's just a small place, and I have never seen anyone other than him go in or out of it."

"Is it true he doesn't speak to his son? I heard Yasuo still works in his father's old *shogi* school, but it's merged or something? Do you know anything about that?"

Sal nodded. "Yeah, that's a sad story, actually. It appears the acquittal didn't make much difference to his family or many others. He was basically run out of Kamakura, even though he originally moved back into the family home after they let him out of jail."

Sal lowered the driver's side window and rolled himself a cigarette.

"Yasuo, he was about fifteen or so at the time, and he seems to have never forgiven his father for what happened to the family. He blamed him for how his mother died and all the family's affairs and disruption. He maintained that his mother would never have had her affair if it wasn't for the father's behavior and that her death had happened because of this. All his fault, in short.

"Anyway, things never got better, and there was never any burying of hatchets. The local *shogi* community and all his neighbors shunned him, so eventually he moved here."

"Does he have a job? How does he live?" asked Penelope.

"He does some online writing work, I think, mainly about *shogi* and under a *nom de plume,* and sometimes he has a gig as a security guard at a local warehouse, but it's just a part-time thing. Money has been tight for him for a long time, and his legal expenses were pretty big."

"Did he get any compensation from the government? You know, for being wrongly imprisoned?"

Sal nodded. "Yeah, he got a few million yen. Not much. It wouldn't have lasted him very long. Anyway, the son merged the old *shogi* school with another larger school. He's a very strong player, probably at least as good as his father. He still works full-time as a *shogi* trainer in Kamakura. Never married, and no kids. I'm wondering if that had something to do with the father as well…."

Penelope sighed. In conservative Japan, where marriage meant both marrying your spouse and their family, it would not be a great leap of the imagination to work out that few families would want their daughter getting involved with anyone who had a father once accused of murder. That would be seen as bad luck for any bride right from the start and associating the family with scandal, something that would not have been seen as appropriate by anyone. Things changed very slowly in this country, she knew.

As they were talking, a light went on and off near the black mailbox, and a shadow appeared on the street walking towards them.

Sal checked his watch.

"Seven-thirty. Right on time, as usual. That's him," he nodded as an older man dressed in a green duffel coat with a small rucksack on his back approached on the other side of the street.

The man had close-cut silver hair and silver-framed glasses. He looked in his mid-sixties and had a pretty powerful build. His eyes were fixed on the pavement in front of him, and he didn't look up even once as he walked briskly past them.

"So that's him…" said Penelope.

Sal nodded. "He's off to the local *shogi* club. He goes there three nights a week. Always the same day and always the same time. He goes in, plays a few games, and leaves on the dot of 9 p.m. He seems to have a lot of friends there. The club is a real working men's *shogi* club, like many places round here. Lots of factory workers and that type, mainly old guys. They know who he is, and they don't care. I think they even like him for it, you know, a bit of notoriety. Sometimes he even goes for a drink with one or two of them at one of the local *izakaya* bars."

Sal started the engine. "Are you ready for a closer look?"

Penelope looked alarmed.

"How are we going to do that?"

Sal smiled. "By playing *shogi* together there. I'm a member."

"Seriously? I don't even know how to play properly," she said. "And what if he spots us?"

Sal turned the car around, and they headed off towards Ikegami station.

"Don't worry. Once he is in there, he hardly looks up from the board. I don't think he even looks at the person he's playing. Just stares at the pieces. I think they give him comfort in a way. We'll be fine. The place is pretty crowded most nights too…."

They went into a small parking station, walked back around the block to a run-down old building, and climbed a dark set of stairs to the third floor, where there was a large metal door with the words 'Ikegami *Shogi* Club' on a large bronze sign.

Penelope felt a flush of cold fear race through her as Sal pushed open the door, but this was soon replaced with a much stronger feeling: claustrophobia. The club was just one long narrow room, with barely enough space to walk down one side of it past the long row of tables that stretched all the way from the door to the far wall. The tables were so close together that they were almost touching, and there was barely enough room for the player sitting in front of the wall to squeeze between them to get into his seat. Each table had an old board with a large plastic box placed neatly in the center, which she knew held the pieces. There were a lot of old faded photographs of various people on the walls in an assortment of cheap frames, and some rather tatty-looking posters advertising long past tournaments and other events.

There was also a battered silver ashtray on every table, and the room was filled with a pall of cigarette smoke. The Tokyo Metropolitan Government had, in a recent fit of enlightenment, imposed strict rules against smoking in places like this, a fact to which they obviously paid precisely zero attention.

Sal paid a small fee to an unshaven old man sitting near the door with a metal cash box, and the man pointed into the room with a gesture that basically meant, 'sit wherever you like.'

They chose to sit near the far end of the room and squeezed their way along the wall to an available table.

Penelope was unsurprised to see that she was the only woman in the room, which was crowded with players, as Sal had said, all grizzled-looking men in their sixties or older, most of whom had an air of quiet despair and cigarettes dangling from their lips as they contemplated their moves.

Glancing about her, she also saw Terumoto sitting against the wall, giving her a clear view of his face. He was about six tables away from them and was sitting on his own with the pieces set up on the board in front of him. He seemed to be waiting for someone, presumably his opponent, and he was lost in thought. He had on an old tan sweater and a checked shirt and looked just like every other man in the club, except for the fact that he was not smoking.

Sal gestured to her that they should set up their pieces and look like they were playing. She began to panic a little though when she realized she had very little idea where the major pieces on the back two rows went, and confused one of the pawns with her rook, which Sal discreetly adjusted for her.

It appeared no one was giving them a second glance in any case.

They began to 'play,' or at least to look like they were playing, and Penelope pushed out some random pieces when Sal whispered to her that she needed to put them on the board in the correct way. She had never done this before and began to wonder if anyone was going to notice that she had, in fact, no idea what she was doing.

To play *shogi* correctly, each piece is held between the index finger and the middle finger and then slapped onto the board with a very audible 'click' with the middle finger.

Penelope couldn't manage to pick the pieces up the correct way, but she did manage to slap them down with enough of a sound to make it look vaguely correct, much to Sal's amusement, who handled the pieces himself like a seasoned professional, much like everyone else in the room. Watching the other players though, she could see a complete difference between even the way Sal did this and the way Terumoto and the more advanced players handled their pieces. These men had a quiet, slow elegance about their actions that she could not quite put her finger on.

She pretended to have a long think over each move, using the time to steal glances at Terumoto, whose opponent had now arrived.

This was a younger man, perhaps in his early forties, with a three-day shadow and slicked-back greasy-looking hair. He was wearing an old sweater and dirty blue jeans and looked like he had not had a bath in some time. He clearly knew what he was doing at the board though, which was probably why Terumoto chose to play him. As the younger man was playing someone who had once been one of the most highly-ranked players in the country, it soon became apparent from the look on his opponent's face and the way he sat shaking his head and scratching his stubble that Terumoto had lost none of his ability.

In the end, the young man gave a short bow and said the traditional word of defeat, *"makemashita"* (I have lost). Terumoto smiled gently and offered him another game, and they set up the pieces again. Penelope noted how the older man sat throughout the game, ramrod straight, his body not touching the back of his chair, perfectly still, almost like he was meditating.

She thought to herself that he didn't look at all like a violent man, a man who could batter a woman to death. Nevertheless, there was the faintest whiff of aggression about him in the last second when he slapped his piece on the board, and a deliberateness that seemed to offer his opponent no quarter.

All around Penelope, the room resounded with the click of pieces hitting the boards and the cloying smoke of cigarettes smoked down to the butt, piling up in ashtrays or hanging forgotten in people's fingers, their dangling willow branches of ash like wilted flowers waiting to fall.

They had been there about an hour when Penelope decided she could stand the place no more, and they made their way outside, where she stood for a while savoring the clean night air on the dark little street, her eyes still stinging and her lungs overworked. She usually did not mind people smoking, even in her own house, where Fei always had her pipe, but this was the first occasion in a long while where she had felt it had been too much.

They got back in Sal's car and returned to their previous place along the road from Terumoto's house to wait for his return.

"He won't be too long," said Sal. "As I said, he's pretty much like clockwork. He'll finish that game around nine-thirty or ten at the latest, and then he will be heading straight back here. What did you think about him?"

Penelope contemplated the question for a while.

"He seems sad," she said finally. "I can feel like he's lost something very important to him."

Sal nodded. "Well, he has, I guess. He lost his family, his career, everything really. Maybe going to that club and playing *shogi* is the only thing that keeps him going."

Penelope turned to him.

"You still think he did it, don't you?"

Sal regarded the front of the old house.

"The wife? Yes. I do. I think he killed her so he could be free to have other women. He was tired of her, and he maybe knew she had her own affairs."

"Why not just divorce her then? Why kill her?"

Sal thought for a while. "That's something that's bothered me too. Two reasons I can think of. Number one was that he was running a *shogi* school, and a divorce might be something that would cause a scandal and badly affect the business. Not much of a reason to kill someone, but I think it's high up on the list. Number two is a bit more psychological and probably won't make much sense, but he is a chess player, and chess is a game of war. He was playing that game with his wife, I think. They both had their affairs, and the marriage was shot. Who was going to win? And don't forget, if they divorced, she would probably get the boy, and that kid was the heir to his *shogi* world."

Penelope stared straight ahead.

"That's even sadder."

Sal nodded. "It is, isn't it."

They waited in silence after that, and a little after ten, just as Sal had predicted, the lonely shape of a man could be seen in the mirror, walking up the road behind their car. He had his little rucksack on his back, and his hands were shoved in the pockets of his trousers. He stared at the ground without looking up as he walked, then turned into his house and went inside. They heard the door click shut quite audibly on the quiet street, and a glimmer of light appeared in one of the downstairs windows.

A dog could be heard barking somewhere. Was it his? Penelope didn't think so. He seemed to be a man with no form of companionship in the whole world.

They drove back to Kamakura, and she invited Sal in for something to drink and eat.

They both had a glass of beer and sat at her living room table as before.

"OK. Let's forget the wife for a minute and just assume for a moment that Terumoto killed her," said Penelope. "That leaves the other killer, who we know dispatched the Enamotos and Watanabe, the other *shogi* master. Those killings are all related to the first one. But why? What's the point of killing those people? All it does is make Terumoto look innocent. But who is going to do that for him? The son was way too young. And why come back eighteen years later and start it all up again, when you got away with the first killings and are home free? Do you *want* to get caught? It seems a bit like a death wish to me, especially knocking off a senior police officer. That's never going to be forgotten by the police. Ever."

Sal topped up her beer glass.

"Yep, you are absolutely right. That's exactly the same road I have been going down. And again, I have no idea why they would reappear and start it again. It's just crazy."

Penelope looked up at him steadily.

74

"No. It's not crazy. That's the last thing it is. It's planned. Planned down to the very last detail. And that's what a *shogi* player would do, right?"

"Yes. That's exactly what a *shogi* player would do. They would be looking down the road at all their options, at what any move they made might provoke in the future. That's how they think."

Penelope sipped her beer and looked at him in a concerned way.

"I agree. Someone planned this very carefully. And they haven't finished."

Chapter 7

Dinner and a Game

From her house, which was located in the Onaricho area, west of the main Kamakura station, Fei and Penelope decided they would walk to their dinner party at Mari's house rather than take a taxi. It was perhaps only thirty minutes or so, and both of them felt like getting outside and into the evening air. The nights were getting cooler now that September was drawing to a close, and the cherry trees were now full of golden leaves as the autumn approached.

They made their way through the quiet little streets, which began to rise as they approached the hills. The houses in these areas were older but much larger than the ones further down, often with substantial gardens surrounded by high wooden walls. They passed by the ancient Kaizo-ji temple, its bell tower and gardens in darkness, and turned into the little lane that led to Mari's house, which as she had said, was not at all far from their friend Suwamoto.

As they expected, it was an old wooden two-storey residence like most of the homes up here, but even in the twilight they could see it had an old garden with several maple trees, a number of stone lanterns lit with little tea candles, and an old pond surrounded by large ornamental rocks.

Suzume let them into the house, dressed in a pretty blue sundress with a butterfly pattern and her shoulder-length hair seemed to shine in the light of the entranceway.

"So pleased you could make it, just come right in," said Mari, appearing next to Suzume. She was wearing old blue jeans and a sweater, and was wiping her hands on an old towel that smelled of turpentine and paint. "Sorry, I was just working on something. I probably stink of paint like everything else in this house."

"Don't worry though, you get used to it after a while. I did," said Suzume, coming to her defense with a smile.

Seeing them standing next to each other like this both dressed in Western clothes, Penelope could see the clear family resemblance between them.

They went down a long hallway into one of the main rooms and saw that the entire back of the house had been extended into the gardens with a glass conservatory, which was presumably where Mari painted so she could make use of the natural light. All of the other rooms were covered with tatami mats, but large oriental-style rugs lay everywhere and the furniture was a mix of Swedish-style leather armchairs and old Japanese cabinets and chests.

Dinner was at a large wooden table next to the modern kitchen, which had been laid for four.

"OK, disclaimer," said Mari. "I didn't cook any of this. I sent Suzume to the department store this morning and that's about all. I am hopeless in the kitchen and find cooking just gets in the way. Suzume cooks though, thank

God. I've never eaten better than since she got here," she smiled.

"Don't worry about it," said Fei. "I hate cooking too. My aunt does everything, so I never darken the kitchen door. I think it's a good arrangement if you live with someone who cooks, actually. Maybe it's the best of both worlds."

Suzume smiled. "Oh, I don't mind cooking. My mother taught me, up in Akita. She cooks everything from scratch. But I only made the rice tonight, the rest is coming from the microwave."

"Department store food from the microwave is my go-to as well for dinner parties," said Penelope, who never shopped there but felt she should say something, even though Fei shot her an astonished look as she uttered this polite and very British untruth.

"Go ahead and smoke Fei-san, if you want. I will, I promise you," said Mari as she lit a cigarette. "Why don't you two have a game of *shogi* before dinner. I'll borrow Penny-*sensei* and show her my studio."

Fei smiled and Suzume took her into the big tatami-mat living room where a large antique *shogi* table was set up ready to play with cushions on either side.

Fei settled on a cushion and picked up one of the pieces.

"These are very nice. *Moriage-goma*? said Fei, referring to a style of engraving where the lacquer is put into the engraved character on the *koma* or piece so that it rises slightly above the surface of the wood. Pieces in this style were usually only used for important title matches.

Suzume nodded. "Yes, Mari-san bought them for my birthday. However, the board has been in the family for a very long time. She used to use it herself when she was young, so she tells me."

"She used to play?"

"Yes, but not anymore. Would you like to be *sente*?"

Fei accepted the traditional role of the guest being the player who moved first, and moved her rook's pawn one square forward with the same elegant movement and sharp 'click' that Penelope had observed with the other advanced players she had seen in the old club in Ikegami the other night on her visit with Sal. The atmosphere in this old Japanese room though, and especially with two women players, was completely different.

Suzume sat in the formal *seiza* position with their legs folded under her, as did Fei, both bolt upright with their backs straight, and they reached out over the board with elegant arm movements without leaning forward, just the same as if they had been wearing kimono for a formal match. Even though Penelope was a veteran of the tea ceremony and was used to sitting in *seiza* herself for long periods, she could not manage more than an hour before her legs were completely numb and cramping would set in, and then like most of her friends she would give in and sit with her legs folded next to her or get up and go for a walk to relieve the pain.

In formal matches, *shogi* required players to sit in the position for sometimes over eight hours straight. They did get up for breaks quite often, but it was pretty normal to see a player sit for an hour or more without moving, something which was a kind of lost ability these days and quite impossible for most people.

Penelope stood by the doorway and watched them play for a while, and Mari fetched them all some glasses of wine.

"Yamada's Climbing Silver'…" said Fei with a smile as Suzume made a familiar series of opening moves. "That seems to be in the news these days. Do you often use this opening? I know I do…."

Suzume smiled. "Yes, I know. I checked out some of your games in my database. You use this one a lot, I saw."

"Oh dear," said Fei. "You have a database? If I had known you were going to check me out I wouldn't have had that glass of wine with lunch. Or this one…" she smiled. Anyway, let's see what you can do…."

Mari gave Penelope a nudge. "Why don't you and I leave them to it? What do you think?"

Mari took Penelope to the rear of the house where the big conservatory jutted into the garden. It was, as she suspected, her studio, and like most artists' studios, it was littered with easels, canvases, and other art equipment.

There was a large wooden table piled high with drawings and other paraphernalia, and Mari offered her an old wooden chair to sit on next to it.

"Wow," said Penelope. "So this is where you paint? I haven't been to a real artist's studio before. So much more interesting than a writer's study. I've had my fill of them over the years. It feels so much more creative…."

Mari nodded. "Yeah, this is where I spend my days. It's a big step up from what I had when I knew you at university. All I had in those days was my bedroom in the house I shared with the other students."

She waved her hands around in the air.

"Art is super messy. You need a bit of space, especially for painting. Canvas takes up a lot of room everywhere. You said you were still writing?"

Penelope nodded. "Every day. I do a little. Not like I used to do, though."

She nodded. "I don't have to paint these days, not if I don't want to. But I can't stop. The moment I see this room in the morning, I end up starting something, and when I look up, it's dinner time. You probably know what that's like."

She picked up a large sketchbook and opened it to a new page.

"Do you mind if I draw you while we talk?"

Penelope smiled. "Sure. If you want to. Though I don't think you are going to get excellent results. Bad subject matter...."

"I need to do something with my hands all the time. It's a bit of a fetish of mine," Mari said as she balanced the book on her lap and began to sketch, drawing lines with a quick, well-practiced hand.

"How is Suzume settling into life in Kamakura? Does she miss her family?" she asked.

"Yeah, she seems fine," said Mari, glancing back and forth between her drawing and Penelope. "All that kid wants to do is play *shogi*. I tell you, it's not a game; it's a bloody *disease*. Once you start, it seems to take you over. It's a lot like this, actually," she said, gesturing to the room around her. "So we get on fine. I have my obsessions, and she has hers. We meet at mealtimes, but we both have completely separate interests. Still, it's nice to have her around. She's been dying to play Fei, actually. I didn't know, but she's apparently quite famous. You knew that, right?"

"Fei? Well, Maybe. *Shogi*'s not really my thing. My friends have told me several times that she is pretty well-known. She and one of our other friends, Yamashita-san, have a *shogi* night once a month or so, sometimes at my house. He's quite a high-level player himself,"

Mari nodded. "Can you just turn your face, just a little… that's right. And just look up slightly. Wonderful… is that chief inspector Yamashita?"

Penelope tried to do as she was told, but it felt a little unnatural to be having a conversation while someone was drawing you.

"Yes. Do you know him?" she said, surprised.

Mari shuffled slightly on her chair.

"I know *of* him," she said. "I saw his name in the paper. So he is a good friend of yours?"

Penelope nodded and then remembered not to move.

"Yes, We've known each other for many years. He is like my big brother in a way. However, I am sure he wouldn't be happy if he heard me say that. I'm older than him by quite a bit, you know."

Mari was staring at her drawing intensely now and not looking at her.

"So he's the one in charge of this latest, what do they call it? *Shogi* Ripper thing? I seem to remember that from a long time ago. After I graduated, I think. There were a bunch of killings, and now another one? It's a bit disconcerting, right? That it's started again. I'm wondering what to do with Suzume, she's with all those *shogi* people all the time. A lot of them are a bit weird, I think. I was one of them myself ages ago… can't say I miss it…."

Penelope watched her drawing rapidly out of the corner of her eye.

"Yamashita-san is in charge of it as far as I know. They have no idea who did the latest killing. Just that it seems to be the same person."

"Why do they think that?" Mari asked.

"Oh, they got a letter. It's the same as the other letters they got years ago."

"But how do they know someone else didn't write it?" Mari sat up and looked her in the eyes again.

"I guess they have their ways. They tested it or something, I believe."

"I guess they did," she said. "It's amazing how much you can tell about someone from their brushstrokes. The way they paint, I mean. You can even tell if they were hungover or just having a bad day… So, you don't think they are any further along in catching them?"

"It doesn't look like it," said Penelope. "I think Yamashita-san is quite upset about it. He was close to the last victim."

Mari carefully tore the sheet of paper out of the sketchbook and passed it to Penelope.

"Here you go, a present for you. I will sign it, and then you can sell it for, I dunno… about a hundred yen," she laughed.

"That's the same as a bottle of water. I bet I could get more down the road at your big fan, Suwamoto-san. It's amazing, thank you. You've even managed to make me look halfway attractive!"

The portrait was incredibly lifelike and showed a very high level of draftsmanship. The way it caught Penelope's eyes and facial expression and the way she had drawn her shoulder-length silver hair had an elegant, sensual quality about it, like in her other paintings of women.

"I think I'm going to get this framed. It's lovely. Thanks so much," said Penelope, quite moved.

They went back into the living room, where Fei and Suzume, were having a post-mortem on the game they had just played. Fei was showing her her some alternative ideas to what she had used, and Suzume was asking her opinion on different pawn structures and other strategies.

"This is all over my head," said Mari. "Let's have some more wine, and I'll serve the food."

Penelope lingered by the living room door, and Suzume got up to go and help her aunt in the kitchen.

"So, how was she?" asked Penelope.

Fei nodded approvingly. "She's very strong. I barely got away with my life. I don't think she would have any problems playing in the professional leagues. She has a fine understanding of the game. I asked her about some things… past famous games. She knew them all. Very impressive."

"That's great. But you are getting on a bit now," Penelope teased.

Fei smiled. "Something I have in common with you, I believe…."

They went into the kitchen and helped lay out the plates.

=====================

"You're very quiet," said Fei, as they walked home afterward.

They were passing through the quiet little streets late at night, and the world was cool and still after the rain and good for walking.

"I was just thinking," said Penny.

"Thinking about what?"

"I dunno, thinking about the Ripper mainly."

"It's a nice evening. Why do you want to think about him for?"

"I'm not sure. Just something Mari said that got me wondering."

"What did she say?"

"She was asking about whether they were any further ahead with finding him, how things were going in the case. And in the process, she called him … 'them', and that got me wondering."

"About grammar?" Fei teased.

"No… about whether the Ripper may be a woman."

Fei put her arm on hers.

"Seriously? Do you know how rare serial killers are in Asia? And do you know how many of them are women?"

"I take it you are going to tell me they aren't like, that common…." Penelope suggested.

Fei shook her head. "Like hen's teeth. That's how common."

Penelope sighed. "Yeah, I know. You're right. It's just that I dunno, we seem not to be looking at all the possibilities here. That's why many of these people get away with it in the past. Other Rippers."

"Other Rippers? Like whom?"

Penelope raised her eyebrows. "You've heard of the Yorkshire Ripper?"

"Vaguely."

"Well, I'm British, so I do. He killed, I think, around fourteen people. That they know of. The search for him was the biggest, in British history. Like this Ripper case here…

"But a woman?"

"All I'm saying is that we need to keep an open mind. If you invest bucketloads of time, money, and effort following a particular theory, you tend not to want to look at others. Particularly the more offbeat," Penelope said, rummaging in her bag for her keys.

They were now standing outside her house.

"Well, goodnight," said Fei. "I'll tell Yamashita what you said when I see him tomorrow. You know he always listens to you. I have no idea why, though!"

Penelope laughed, and they parted at her front gate, and Fei went into her house next door, where she heard her talking to her aunt in the quiet of the evening.

She opened her front door and found all four of her cats lined up, waiting to say hello and, more importantly, to get their dinner.

"Well, hello, guys. You must be hungry."

She dropped her bag on the floor and turned to close the door when she noticed a shadowy form moving on the other side of her little street. It was too dark to make out who it was, and she could only see their back, but it was an older man with close-cut hair and wearing a duffel coat and old blue jeans. He walked hunched forward with his head down, staring at the road ahead with his hands in his pockets. The figure walked rapidly to the corner of the street and then disappeared.

For a split second, she caught her breath. It could be anyone, but… it was so similar…

Terumoto?

The same duffel coat, t-he same jeans, the same way of walking…

What was he doing here?

The answer came quickly enough to her, though.

He's here for you…

She shut the door with a bang and, with shaking hands, bolted it.

Chapter 8

The Yorkshire Profile

The next morning Sal was sitting in her kitchen smoking a cigarette and drinking coffee. He was wearing his usual old, checked workman's shirt and jeans, and looked like a down-on-his-luck graduate student rather than a reasonably famous writer and journalist. Not that anyone clearly knows what one of those was supposed to look like these days.

Kamakura is a small town, and he lived not too far away from Penelope in an old ramshackle house he had inherited from his parents, which he occasionally shared with his sister, a struggling actress who seemed to have no fixed abode and wandered all over the country wherever there was work in the theatre or on TV or doing voiceovers. He had a couple of elderly cats to whom he was devoted, and spent nearly every waking moment working on some book, article, or other piece to scrape together enough money to live.

Unable to sleep, Penny had sent him a text the night before and asked him over for what she liked to refer to as 'morning tea,' a ritual she indulged most days as a sort of forlorn homage to her waning Britishness. Her national identity, it seemed, had long since morphed into something halfway between being Japanese and being just vaguely 'foreign,' and was something she was almost entirely unaware of most of the time, and the only occasions it came back to her with any degree of certainty was when she met other British people who had not been long enough in Japan to acclimatize to the degree she had.

However, this morning her purpose was not simply to catch up with a friend over Twining's Orange Pekoe tea and scones but rather to put to rest an idea that had been building in the back of her head for some days. This idea stemmed from a growing feeling that if they were ever going to solve this mystery, they needed to head in a new direction, to whit, a direction the police had not previously considered. To understand whether her rather radical thesis was correct or not, she needed a friendly and informed ear with which to bat the idea around a little, and Sal would do.

Sal had said he was free and had turned up on the dot of ten o'clock as proposed, and Penelope had not even served the scones before she turned to the subject of the case.

She had decided not to tell him about the figure she had seen outside her house last night. It was probably nothing, just some old guy out for a walk, and her overactive imagination had immediately put two and two together and got fifteen. It was not worth talking about and she felt a bit ashamed of herself for letting her imagination run away with her, so she decided simply to press ahead.

Sal had listened attentively as he waited for his tea to cool, but his first response was not encouraging.

"A woman?" he said meditatively as he looked out over the vegetable garden.

Penelope nodded, and Sal looked at her with interest, not a little skepticism.

"Why would you suggest *that,* Penny-*sensei*," he asked with a serious air.

Penelope sat down in her usual old wicker chair opposite him and clasped her hands together in front of her. The morning sunlight was streaming across the garden and a large, orange-breasted thrush was warming itself on the passionfruit trellis and looking in on them as if to report their conversation later for the amusement of his feathered friends.

"It's just a feeling, really. You know me, I've read a lot of mysteries. It just seems to me that when the police have no luck finding the killer, it's often because they are heading off down the wrong road. And the longer they are on that road, the more reluctant they are to change their thinking and look at the case in a fresh way. To tell you the truth, I really get the feeling that's what is happening here, right? I mean, let's face it. From what I can gather from you and Yamashita-san, this case has been a total dead-end from the beginning. Like a lot of other cases overseas in the past involving serial killers. Would I be right in saying that?" she asked.

Sal looked at the floor. "Yeah, I guess so. Sure. To be honest...that's probably about where we are. Like nowhere..."

"OK, then. Let's just think about this. The other day I was telling Fei about the Yorkshire Ripper. I'm sure you know that case, right?"

Sal nodded and lit another cigarette.

"Hell, yes, of course. It's one of the most famous. A lot of policing changed because of the mistakes made in that one. That was back in the good old days before DNA and profiling too. It's in all the textbooks, not to mention there is a swathe of books in your local library on it which all make a lot more money than mine."

"Well, he killed a lot more people," offered Penelope consolingly. "The point I am making, though, is that in the long hunt for the Yorkshire Ripper, who ended up being a sort of non-entity truck driver called Peter Sutcliffe, the police in Britain interviewed tens of thousands of people. And in the process, they had said Peter Sutcliffe in the police station for interviews on at least *nine* different occasions."

"Yes, I did read that somewhere," said Sal.

"And the reason they never arrested him? Because all that time they had this set-in-cement profile of what kind of person the killer was supposed to be, a profile that was completely wrong by the way, and so each time he just walked away and killed someone else."

"That's all true," said Sal, "and I see what you're saying; however, first of all, regarding the *Shogi* Ripper, you're going to have to show me *where* the current police profile is wrong. Because, as far as I can see, it's pretty logical. It's a guy, he must be in his late forties or fifties, physically strong, and with some connection to *shogi*. Seems pretty bang on to me. Anyway, what makes you think it's a woman? Do you know how rare that is? In Asia?"

Penelope nodded. "I know, I know. Fei told me. I'm not saying it *is* a woman, either. I just think we need to look at things with a broader view."

"Fei-san is right, however. Women usually don't batter someone to death with a hammer. That's not the usual female MO," he said.

"True. Unless maybe the killer *wants* you to think she's a man. Let's not forget people like Lizzie Borden and several others I could mention, who were not at all shy about using extreme physical violence. But let's assume it's just a normal woman, not someone possessed of enormous physical strength or anything. Let's just think about it for a minute. If a woman wants to kill a fine physical specimen of a man… like you, for example, what does she have to do?"

Sal grinned. "Besides buy me a drink?"

"Yes. Or slipping something into your morning tea."

Sal eyed his cup and looked up. "I guess she would have to make sure I wasn't able to fight back."

Penelope slapped her knee.

"That's my point. A woman is not going to attack a man openly. There's a reason poison is a favorite for women. Or else…some kind of surprise attack."

Sal nodded. "OK, I see where you are going with this. Like, hit him on the head from behind."

Penelope nodded. "Exactly. Like hit him on the head from behind. A woman can do that. A woman can wield a hammer, just like a guy can. And every single victim in this case, all five of them, were initially hit from behind."

"True… but…"

"I know, I know… Asia…Japan… women serial killers. I know all that. But just suppose for a moment. Were any of the bodies moved after they were killed?"

Sal thought for a moment. "No. They were all left where they fell."

"Wouldn't that be consistent with the killer being a person who didn't have the strength to move them?"

Sal laughed. "Yeah…possibly. But maybe there was no need to move them."

"What about the Enamoto couple? You know, the second killing, after Terumoto's wife. How did they die?"

Sal took a sip of his coffee. "She was in the kitchen on the floor and was killed first. It looked like she must have known the killer because there was no sign that the house had been broken into, kinda like Toyozaki's. He might have let the killer in, too. Anyway, with the Enamoto killing, there was also no sign of any quarrel or struggle. Blunt force trauma to the back of the head in the initial attack, as you said, and then a continued assault, no doubt, to ensure the person was dead. The husband came home maybe an hour later, and the same thing happened to him."

"Hit on the back of the head."

"Yes," said Sal. "Both of them."

"So neither of them knew they were going to be attacked. They were both taken unawares. Right?"

Sal nodded.

"What about Watanabe, the *shogi* teacher? He was the last killing eighteen years ago? Same thing, right?"

"Not quite. Well, maybe. His was a little bit different in the sense of where it occurred."

"How do you mean?"

"Well…I'm not supposed to tell you this, I think. The family wanted it kept quiet. He was killed outdoors, in the street, late at night."

"What's so scandalous about that?"

Sal leaned forward.

"He was killed in a little street in Shinjuku full of love hotels. No cameras in those places usually, for obvious reasons."

Penny put her coffee down on the table with a bang.

"Wait a minute… Wait a minute. Before you get all excited about the woman thing, there is something else you should know."

"What was that?"

"He wasn't there with a woman. He liked young guys," said Sal with a slight smile.

"He was gay?"

"Yes. Well, gay or bisexual. But he was definitely tending toward the gay side in his later years. He had kept it under the radar all his life, like many gay men in Japan. And especially men in such a conservative world as *shogi*. His wife and kids never knew a thing about his secret life until after he died. But he was a known entity on the gay scene in Shinjuku and other places. The love hotel he was visiting catered to gay couples almost exclusively," he said, looking up at the ceiling as if remembering something. "It was me that found this out. I kept it out of the book because of his family. His wife was a really nice person, she didn't need any more grief. But the police know, of course. I gave all that information to Toyazaki and others in return for the inside scoop on the case."

"You are a good guy, Sal," Penelope smiled.

"I know. I'm a saint," he grinned. "But unfortunately, even more than the others, Watanabe's death points to a guy."

"True. But he was killed *outside* the hotel, right? That means it might not have been by the guy he was with. That

94

guy could have just killed him inside in the privacy of their room," she said.

Sal nodded. "You're relentless. Yeah. It's true. We never found out who he was with, though. Naturally enough, and given the homophobia rampant in the police department and elsewhere, the guy never came forward. But Watanabe was a different kind of killing too, in other ways."

"How so?"

"Well, obviously, it was outside. In a sleazy little alley on the west side of Ikebukuro station, not a nice place in Tokyo back then. The killer took a big risk killing him in public like that. The body was found just minutes later. So I've always kinda felt that his killing might have been unplanned. A crime of opportunity. Like the killer just took their chance when they saw it."

"Maybe the killer didn't like what they saw. Maybe the thought of him in a love hotel made them furious somehow… Maybe they also have extreme feelings of hatred for gay people."

"That's possible. I've thought about that too. Or it could be just the opposite. A jealous lover. And all of his lovers, and they were numerous by all accounts, were men…."

"OK. That's interesting. Thanks for telling me about that, it gives me something more to think about. A gay man? Someone connected to the *shogi* world? Maybe there is some other connection we are missing?"

Sal nodded. "Well, you're right. And look, I understand where you are coming from, Penny-*sensei*. We *are* definitely missing something. I've always had that feeling too. It's like you get told half of a story and then left to wonder what will happen…."

Penelope sighed. "True. Do you want some more tea? I'm going to have one."

Sal held out his cup.

"Sure. Why not."

Penelope went into the kitchen and emerged a few minutes later to find Sal making friends with Marmalade, her huge orange tabby, who was sprawled in the sun on the tatami mat floor, enjoying having her ears scratched.

"Oh, don't start that. She'll never let you stop," she smiled.

"That's OK, she's welcome. Ah, and here is something else I found out. Are you ready?"

"Of course. Spill the beans," she said as she passed him a mug of tea.

"Guess who doesn't have an alibi for Toyozaki's killing?"

"I have no idea. Who? Me?"

"No, not you. Though you certainly know what you are doing. No, I was thinking of our old friend Terumoto-san."

"Really? How do you know?"

Sal leaned forward.

"This is confidential. You know that old guy on the desk at the *shogi* parlor? Terumoto's second home?"

"Yeah. I remember."

"Well, we have a little arrangement sometimes. Terumoto did not come in that night. And he is always there on a Sunday. He has a regular game."

"You pay that guy?" asked Penelope.

"Occasionally," said Sal with a sly look.

"Wow. The shady world of investigative journalists. I never knew."

"Well," said Sal, "That's the way the world turns. It's all quid pro quo, you know."

"So I see…You still think Terumoto might be involved somehow?"

Sal cocked his head to one side.

"That one… I would never rule him out. I think he's got a nasty side most people don't know about…."

There was a sound of the garden gate opening, and they both looked up as Fei came in down the side of the house via the garden, which was her usual way in and out of Penelope's house.

"Oh, hello, you two. You're in my seat, Sal. Can I have tea too?" she said with a smile as Sal graciously got up and pulled up a kitchen chair for himself.

"So what's the conversation? As if I couldn't guess."

"The usual," said Penelope. "Murder."

Fei laughed and lit her pipe.

"Of course. What else. And has she been haranguing you with her theories again?"

"Something like that," said Sal. "What brings you around, Fei?"

Fei looked at him, confused.

"I live here. I thought you knew that." she leaned forward, "I'm here to invite you, well Penny actually, but you can come too, to watch a *shogi* tournament on Saturday."

"Ah… *shogi* again…" said Sal. "That keeps coming up. Why? Are you playing?"

"No, not me. Someone you don't know. Suzume called me."

"Suzume is our friend," Penelope explained for Sal's benefit. "She plays *shogi*."

"Yes," said Fei. "Anyway, if she wins on Saturday, it will go a long way to help her turn pro. She asked if we could come and lend her some moral support. Want to go?"

Penelope nodded. "Of course, we should do that if it's important to her. I guess Mari will be there too?"

Fei shrugged and smiled. "Yes. I guess so. Anyway, that's the spirit. I thought we should try and turn up too. If she can win, it will be a big moment for her. I kind of understand the pressure."

Penelope knew Fei had been very close to becoming a professional when she was young but decided to listen to her family and go into medicine instead. She often wondered if she regretted that decision when she saw her play. It sometimes seemed that Fei was never calmer and more at ease than when she was sitting in front of a *shogi* board.

Sal sat back and crossed his arms. "Sounds interesting. I haven't been to a *shogi* tournament in years."

"Well, it's a date then. You can drive us if you like. It's in Kamakura."

"Sounds like a plan," said Sal.

They arranged a time to meet, and Sal offered to pick them both up at 9 a.m. the following morning and take them to the playing venue, a large temple on the other side of Kamakura near the sea. *Shogi* tournaments, especially between top players, were often held in temples, shrines, and hotels, so there was nothing unusual about the tournament taking place in such a venue.

Sal and Fei departed for their homes and left Penelope alone to contemplate their conversation. There was one question that really kept playing in her head, and it was not something they had discussed. The question was a straightforward one, but probably something that held the key to the whole mystery, and that was why this killer, after so long, had suddenly come back and struck again. It couldn't, she reasoned, be that they had just gotten bored or had some overwhelming urge to kill again. Otherwise, they would never have stopped in the first place.

No, she reasoned, they had come back because they needed to, and for a specific reason. Nothing else could justify it. Just like they had stopped for a particular reason all those years before. This much, she figured, had to be true.

All she had to do was figure out what that reason was.

Chapter 9

Blood on the Buddha.

The next morning they arrived at the playing center in Sal's ancient and none-too-clean Toyota Landcruiser, with Fei forced to sit in the back seat squashed between the pile of camping equipment, about which discomfort she had plenty to say. The tournament was being held in a large hall attached to a Buddhist temple, and when they arrived there were a lot of spectators crowded into the hall, most of them standing at the back and around the walls. The forty or so players sat at large folding tables with two boards on each evenly spaced around the venue.

Today's games were timed, and the players had forty-five minutes each to make their moves before a thirty-second-per-move extra time was allowed until someone won. Unlike in Western chess, there are no or extremely few draws in a game of *shogi*, so there is nearly always a result for better or worse.

If a player won their game, they would go to the back of the hall and report to the arbiters, who would then collate the results and post their next match on a large board at the side of the room. This being an important tournament, it was only for advanced female players holding the rank of first *dan* or above.

They found Suzume quickly after they went in. She was sitting at the front of the hall, deep in thought and enjoined in a battle with her opponent, another very serious-looking young woman perhaps a few years older than her. Both players were vying to join the professional ranks that day, and the result of this tournament was critical in deciding whether or not that dream would become a reality. Almost nobody in *shogi* could join the professional division if they were over the age of thirty, and most entered when they were in their early to mid-twenties or even younger. The youngest to have achieved this was a girl in her early teens and still in junior high school, which was becoming more and more a feature of how things were going, not only in Japanese chess, but even more so in its Western counterpart.

Penelope saw Mari standing in the corner of the room and made her way over to say hello. The artist wore a simple black sundress today and had a small red backpack. She was standing next to a handsome gentleman in his later thirties in a dark suit with whom she was having a whispered conversation while glancing nervously at Suzume's back some meters away.

"Ah, Penny-*sensei*!" she said on seeing her friend. "That's so sweet of you and Fei to come. This is Yasuo Terumoto, Suzume's teacher."

Penelope smiled, and they exchanged greetings. The man seemed slightly preoccupied but had an easy manner and a warm smile.

"Sorry, but we are all a bit nervous today," said Terumoto. "It's a pretty big day for her," he said, gesturing in Suzume's direction.

Penelope nodded. She could not see a strong family resemblance with his father, no matter how hard she tried. Perhaps the son took after his mother, but he seemed to have a completely different attitude to that of his morose father. Still, she felt something about his looks was a little strange, but it was hard to put her finger on what it was. However, she kept these thoughts to herself, as she didn't really have any way of telling him that she had recently been on a spying expedition staking out his relative.

"Fei said Suzume was a very strong player. I'm sure she'll do well today. Were you a professional yourself, Terumoto-san?" she asked.

Terumoto nodded. "Yes, for about ten years or so. A very minor one. These days I just teach, however. We have a school here in Kamakura," he said without taking his eyes off Suzume.

Penelope followed his gaze and saw he was genuinely nervous for his protégé.

"I've heard about your school from Mari. That's the Okamoto school, is that right?"

"Yes, that's the one. I'm a coach there," he said.

"The head coach," said Mari with an encouraging smile. "Oh, there's Imabara-san. He's just left. I'll be right back," she said, heading toward the doorway.

Penelope and Terumoto watched her go.

"So… You're the head coach? You must be very busy," said Penelope.

"Well, we don't have titles there. But yes, I've been there since I was a boy myself. Old Okamoto-*sensei* trained me."

"Do you come from a *shogi* family yourself, Terumoto-san," she ventured, just to see how he would react.

Terumoto stiffened slightly, but his smile did not leave his lips, but before he could answer, there was a buzzing noise and he reached into his pocket and fished out his mobile phone, where he read a message someone had sent.

"Yes, in a way. But I was always trained in the Okamoto school. Please excuse me for just a moment."

He walked quickly towards the door, and at that moment, Fei and Sal came over, and they chatted for a moment.

A few minutes later, and to their surprise, they saw Suzume stand up and bow to her opponent. The latter did not look at all pleased and was frowning as they both packed away the pieces into their little wooden box and placed it on the table.

Suzume turned and made her way to the arbiter's table, where she had a brief conversation before spotting Fei and Penelope.

"So, is it congratulations?" said Fei. "This is Sal, by the way. He plays too, I hear."

Sal smiled. "Very badly. Nice to meet you, Suzume-san. How was your match?"

Suzume nodded and smiled nervously. "She was really strong," she said, nodding over to where she had just been playing. "I nearly blew it completely at one point. But then she made a mistake and… I was fortunate. If they are all as strong as her, I am going to be toast by the end of the day, I think."

Penelope laughed.

103

"You'll be fine. Just take it one game at a time. When is your next one?"

Suzume looked at her watch. "In about half an hour," she said.

"Do you want to go outside for a breath of fresh air?" asked Fei.

"Sure. That sounds like a good idea. Let's do that."

They walked around the back of the hall and went outside into the sunshine, which felt like going into a different world after the tense atmosphere of the playing hall.

Suzume seemed to be looking around for someone who wasn't there.

"Are you looking for your aunt? She went out for a cigarette." Penelope offered.

"Actually, I was wondering if my coach was here. Yasuo-san. Did you meet him yet?" she asked.

"Yes, I met him, your aunt introduced us. He seems very nice. I think he went out to take a phone call."

Suzume smiled. "OK, I was just wondering where he was. He was more nervous than me yesterday."

At that moment, Mari appeared and joined them, patting her niece on the shoulder.

"You won, I hear! That's wonderful. One down, three to go, right?"

Suzume nodded. "Yes, and then the final, if I make it that far…." she said.

"You will," said Fei. "Have faith."

They all stood outside in the sunshine for a little longer, and then Suzume indicated she had better be getting back inside, so they accompanied her back in and saw her take a seat at one of the other tables in the middle of the hall, where she was soon joined by an older woman in her forties.

"Ah… I know her," said Fei, gesturing towards Suzume's opponent. "That's Sumire Tanaka, I've played her before. She's really solid. I didn't know she still played in tournaments. Suzume will have her work cut out for her with that one," she said, grimacing slightly.

"I think they are all really strong in this tournament," said Mari. "At least that's what her coach told me. It's going to be a long day. Especially for her."

They watched as the two players bowed to each other and then began placing the pieces on the board. At the appointed time, about a minute later, they both started the little clock on the side of the table, which they would touch after every move to keep track of their time.

Penelope looked at Fei. "I don't know how you stand the tension," she said. "I feel so nervous I'm shaking, and I'm not even playing…."

"Me too," said Mari. "I don't have the stomach for these things. It's worse than getting married. Not that I've done that…."

Fei smiled. "You get used to it. She's been doing this since she was a child, just like me. It's OK to feel nervous. Actually, it's good. Once you start playing, the nerves go away, I always found. You just think about the game."

The game had been going for a little over twenty minutes when out of the corner of her eye, Penelope noticed an elderly, black-robed Buddhist priest walk in quickly from outside and march over to the arbiter's table. Whatever he said seemed to cause an instant consternation among the arbiters, and after a brief conversation and they rose and quickly followed the priest out of the hall.

"I wonder what all that was about," said Fei. "They aren't supposed to leave the hall with the games in play. There could be a dispute. At least one of them should have stayed," she frowned.

"Maybe they are organizing lunch," joked Sal. "That would be nice. Unless it's all vegetarian here…" he added in a disappointed tone.

A few minutes later, Penelope, always curious, went over to the doorway and saw the arbiters and the priest standing outside in a circle having what looked like an animated conversation, and then a bald man, whom she took to be the head arbiter, turned and headed back into the hall toward her, ashen-faced and solemn.

The arbiter went to the front of the hall and spoke to everyone in a loud voice.

"Ladies and gentlemen," he began, and Penelope thought his voice shook slightly. "Please stop your clocks. Due to unforeseen circumstances, today's tournament has been cancelled. Your results for the first round will stand until we can reconvene at a later date. I deeply apologize for this inconvenience and ask that you all remain in your seats until we can get a clearer picture of the situation. Unfortunately, a serious crime has been reported on the premises, and the police will be with us shortly, but there is no danger. Please do not leave the hall. I repeat. Players and spectators, please remain in the hall for the time being."

Penelope spun around and caught Fei and Sal's eyes.

"Did he say 'police?" asked Sal.

"He did," replied Fei.

All the players had stopped their games, and many of the spectators moved to be with them while they waited. Suzume and her opponent had packed away the pieces, and she now came over and joined her aunt, where they stood waiting for some idea as to what had happened.

Fei turned to Sal and Penelope and whispered.

"Come with me."

The three went over to the door where the arbiters were standing, and Fei had a brief conversation with the head arbiter, who gestured that they could leave the building if they wished.

"What did you tell him?" said Penelope as they emerged outside.

"I told him I work with the police, and you were with me," she smiled slyly.

Sal laughed. "Well, that's true in a way."

"I know," said Fei. "Anyway, let's see if we can find out what's going on."

As she spoke, there were the sounds of a siren from somewhere close by, and three sweating policemen on bicycles appeared at the gate leading into the temple. The priest who had been talking to the arbiters earlier rushed over to them and gestured for them to follow him into the main hall of worship.

Fei followed them, and Penelope and Sal trailed behind her. She had a brief conversation with one of the police officers who had posted himself at the door, and after showing him her ID card the officer waved her in and Penelope and Sal simply followed her with the officer, not giving them a second glance.

Inside the main hall it was quite dark as the outer shutters were still pulled down due to the hall not being in use at that moment. The room was lit with small electric candles and flickering lamps arranged around a large golden statue of the Buddha, serene on a large wooden pedestal and surrounded by ornate gold decorations. As they moved into the main room, the object of all the consternation appeared before them.

They were not able to see clearly from where they stood, but the priest and the three policemen were standing over the body of what appeared to be a man in a dark suit lying face down on the wooden floor of the hall in front of the Buddha statue. The man was lying in a pool of his own blood with his face turned away from them, and the back of his head was a bloody mess. A large sheet of clear plastic lay beside him, also covered in blood. Whoever, the man, was, he was very clearly dead.

The policeman turned and beckoned to Fei.

"Are you the medical examiner?" he asked.

Fei nodded. "You should get out of here and wait for forensics. I'll look at the body after they're finished," she said.

The officers looked at each other and agreed, and they all left the building and went outside again, where two squad cars had now arrived, and several other officers were heading into the player's hall.

"Wow," said Sal. "Who do you think that was?"

Penelope had her suspicions but decided to keep them to herself. "No idea, but I think we are about to find out. I better go back and see Mari and Suzume, they must be wondering what's happening."

Sal followed her back inside while Fei went to talk with the arriving police.

She quickly found Mari with Suzume standing by her side in the hall, looking around nervously.

"I'm so glad you came back," said Mari. "What's going on? Are we going to get out of here anytime soon, do you think?"

"Hmmm… I don't know. It's a bit complicated, I'm afraid."

Suzume touched her on the arm.

"Have you seen my coach, Yasuo-san? He's not here. It's strange, he promised me he would be here for my match," she said agitatedly.

Penelope could see something was clearly wrong with her, and she began to get an aching feeling in the pit of her stomach when she thought about what she had just seen in the temple. It had not been possible to get more than a glance at the body, and she had not been able to see the face at all, but now Suzume had mentioned her coach, she remembered that he had also been wearing a dark suit. She decided not to pre-empt things and worry her by mentioning what she had seen.

"Well, the last I saw of him, he went outside to answer his phone. Maybe he had to go somewhere. Anyway, don't worry about him now," she said soothingly. "Do you have a moment, Mari-san?"

She drew Mari aside, and they walked over to the door together.

"Look, Mari-san," she began. "Don't tell Suzume this, but they found a body in the temple. That's why all the police are here. They will probably want to interview everyone, so it might be a while before we can leave."

Mari's eyes widened. "A body? You mean someone is dead?"

She nodded. "It's a murder, I'm afraid."

"Oh my God. Do you know who it is?" she asked, glancing in her niece's direction.

Penelope shook her head. "No idea, sorry," she said. But the image of Yasuo Terumoto was more and more taking shape in her mind, and a cold fear blew through her when she thought of Suzume.

About twenty minutes later, there was a murmur of voices from the doorway, and the familiar face of Chief Inspector Yamashita appeared, followed by Fei. Seeing Penelope, he gave her a brief nod of greeting and then made his way to the front of the hall.

He raised his hands for silence, and the hall fell quiet.

"Ladies and gentlemen. I want to apologize for this inconvenience. I regret to inform you that there has been a death in the facility we are currently investigating. Because this death is suspicious, we are unfortunately going to have to speak to each of you before you leave today. I would appreciate it if you could give the officers a few minutes of your time to answer some questions, and again, I apologize for any delays or inconvenience this causes you. Thank you in advance for your co-operation. Please remain within the hall."

He turned and headed out the door again, and Penelope watched him talking to the arbiters in the lobby.

She turned to Fei, who was standing by her side.

"Any news?" she asked.

Fei sighed. "Yes. I'm afraid so…" She turned to Mari and touched her on the arm.

"I'm sorry, but we need to talk to Suzume, I'm afraid," she said quietly.

Mari looked at her, confused. "Suzume? Why?"

"I'm afraid the person who died… is her coach. Terumoto-san."

Mari's hand flew to her mouth in shock. "What?" she whispered.

Sal swore, and Penelope stared over at where Suzume was standing, looking at her phone.

"Are you sure it's him?" asked Sal.

Fei nodded. "I'm afraid so. We haven't formally identified the body, but that's what it said in the wallet we found. And I met him, remember? It's definitely him. I'm sorry. This is going to be quite a shock for her; I suggest we tell her before she finds out from one of these police officers or starts putting two and two together. Bring her out to the lobby. I'll tell her. Then take her home. I'll clear it with the Chief Inspector, he's an old friend."

Mari shook her head sadly and went over to Suzume, where she had a brief word, and together the four of them took the worried-looking girl out to the lobby.

Fei made her sit on one of the folding chairs near the arbiter and told her professionally but kindly what had happened to her coach.

Suzume looked at her uncomprehendingly for a moment. Then she fainted on the floor.

Chapter 10

Post-Mortem

Dear little policemen,

Well, here I am again. As usual, I am free, and as usual, you have no idea who I am, do you?

What a shame… that must be such a frustrating feeling.

I must admit, it's been fun to get back into action again after my long sleep… and I really feel invigorated about starting again.

Anyway, I'm not yet sure how many people are going to die, but I think at least a few more need to finish their days. I don't really care who they are, of course, that's not what motivates me.

It's time to take another member of the 'T' family. Can you guess who that is?

Good luck!

Your friend,

CS.

Yamashita sighed while Sal, Penelope, and Fei read the letter. They were once again gathered around Penelope's kitchen table after she had offered to make Yamashita another meal, and she had asked Sal to join them again as Yamashita had said he would value his input.

"We got that the day before the last killing, and it wasn't even twenty-four hours before we had another body. This time it was sent to me by post at the police station, postmarked the previous day, and mailed from one of maybe a dozen post boxes around the city. The only one with a camera on it was the one in front of the main Kamakura Post Office, where of course, there was no footage anyway because the camera hasn't worked for a year. Whoever this is, it's beginning to feel like they are killing on a timetable. Like they are in a hurry."

Fei, who had conducted the autopsy on Terumoto-san, sat back down and lit up her pipe.

"It does rather feel like that, doesn't it? Did you find anything at the crime scene?" she asked.

Yamashita should his head. "Not a bean. No prints. No DNA. Nothing… as usual.

"What about the priest?" asked Penelope. "Where was he at the time?"

"The priest? He had popped into the hall to watch the *shogi* for a minute. Apparently, he is a bit of a fan, and they have staged some major tournaments in the past at the temple, some title matches for professional players. It seems that the temple has been involved in *shogi* for a long time."

"So he saw nothing?" asked Sal.

Yamashita shook his head.

"No, nothing at all. He walked through the temple on the way to the hall. Nothing unusual, and when he walked back about thirty minutes later, he found the body."

"I see. Well, at least you have a pretty exact time of death."

"We do. That's about all, though," said Fei.

"The killer did one thing that was new, however," said Yamashita.

"What was that?" asked Penelope.

"Well, and this is weird," began Yamashita. "He hit him on the head with what looks like the usual hammer, and then when he was on the floor, he covered the head with a piece of clear plastic and finished him off."

"That's right. There were five blows in all. One without the plastic and then four heavy blows through it," said Fei. "It looked like the wounds were made with a common builder's hammer that you could buy in any hardware store or online. Same as all the other victims. The plastic was a new touch, however. That kind of plastic is hard to rip, especially if you hit something underneath it that's soft. Like someone's head…."

They were all silent for a moment, trying to understand what this meant.

"Well, that's charming… thanks, Fei. I'm glad you waited until after we had all eaten. Why would he do that, do you think? The plastic?" asked Penelope.

Fei and Yamashita both threw up their arms.

"The only reason I can think of would be to reduce the blood spatter at the scene," said Yamashita.

Penelope nodded and folded her arms meditatively.

"So the plastic would have acted to concentrate the blood spatter in one place," she said.

"That's all I can come up with. You're welcome to propose another theory. The priest said the plastic sheet didn't belong to them, so the killer must have brought it with them. It's the kind you can find in any '100-yen shop', the kind of thing people take with them on picnics as a small ground sheet to sit on," said Yamashita, taking a sip of his wine.

"So… the first blow… there is no blood spatter from that?"

Fei shook her head. "The first blow would have knocked him out, not necessarily killed him. The blood spatter comes after that, usually when you repeatedly hit the head, smashing the skull. There's not necessarily any blood spatter from the initial blow."

Penelope and Sal looked at each other.

"So… the killer would have known that," said Sal.

"Yes," said Yamashita. "This guy has form. He knows exactly what he is doing."

"So it might also make sense to say that the killer could have used the sheet because he didn't want to get any blood on himself, right?" asked Penelope.

"Yep, that's a possibility. Or simply because this person is completely nuts and just felt like doing it that way. Which I do not believe, by the way…." said the chief inspector.

Penelope shook her head. "Neither do I. But there is one logical conclusion you might be able to draw, and that is that the killer didn't want any blood on them because it would have been noticed, and it would have been noticed because… they were there. In the playing hall."

Yamashita stared at her thoughtfully.

"That's also a possibility."

"So, no one left the hall? You interviewed them all?" asked Sal.

Yamashita nodded. "Of course. No one left, and no one was reported as leaving before we got there."

"Of course, the other side of this is that they might not have been in the playing hall at all. They might have been waiting in the temple the whole time or come from outside somewhere. Remember, Terumoto got a phone call while he was in the hall, and then he went to the temple, presumably to meet whoever made the call to him," said Fei

"Yes, that's absolutely right. Of course, we checked the phone, and the call came from a burner phone that was somewhere within a three-kilometer radius of the temple, and that's all we know about it. The call only lasted about fifteen seconds. Very short. I'm wondering if he knew who it was from, which would make him go into the temple," said Yamashita. "That's only a theory, of course....."

"What Fei said is true," said Penelope. "It could have been either. Someone not wanting blood on them because they were going back to the playing hall, or someone not wanting blood on them because they were going back out onto the street. Whichever way, if you kill someone in broad daylight, you don't want to be seen with blood on you. It might even mean you would wear something dark, just in case."

"Also, you would have to have some kind of a bag to transport the murder weapon and presumably the plastic sheet. If that were a hammer, as you guys As you guys suspect, if that were a hammer, just about any bag would do the job," added Sal. "With a killer this careful, I can't imagine them leaving it at the scene. They've never done that before."

Yamashita nodded. "That's all true. It just doesn't help a lot. My money would be on it being someone from outside, not someone connected to the *shogi* tournament. You would be taking a hell of a risk otherwise."

"That's true," said Penelope. "Killing someone in that brutal way and then popping back into a crowded hall and pretending like nothing happened. That takes nerves…."

Sal picked up the photocopy of the letter Yamashita had brought and held it up.

"This letter is of a piece with all the other letters from eighteen years ago and the one you showed us a few weeks ago from the Toyozaki killing. It's the same tone, language, brush, ink…everything," he said.

"Yes, it's identical. That's what the graphologists say too. Exactly the same person wrote all these letters," said Yamashita.

Sal stared at the piece of A4 paper in his hands.

"Why does he add this bit about 'I don't care who they are…" he asked.

Yamashita shrugged, "I know. That struck me as odd too."

"Why?" asked Fei.

"Because…" interjected Penelope. "They *are* all connected. They are all from a select pool of people. They are all connected by *shogi*, and/or they were investigating the case. I wonder if that is why he used the word 'family' in the letter as well."

"That's a good point, " said Sal quietly. "So he obviously *does* care who they are. This isn't random."

Yamashita nodded in agreement. "Exactly what I thought. He says this because he wants us to *think* it's random. Which makes him more difficult to find."

"Absolutely," said Sal. "Which means you have a problem coming, maybe."

"What do you mean?" said Fei. "I thought we had a problem now...."

"Well, all the victims had something in common, either *shogi*, or the case. What if the future victims, presuming they occur, actually *are* random?"

They were all silent for a while.

"Then we assume one of two things," said Penelope. "We assume they are red herrings, and we disregard them and focus on the connected victims, or...."

"Or what?" said Sal.

"Or we keep digging until we find some connection," she said. "More wine, anyone?"

Yamashita and Fei held out their glasses.

"That's logical, but it's a rather risky approach. I would rather assume any future victim had some connection than not," said Yamashita

"Which may be precisely what he wants you to think, so we go chasing our tails for another eighteen years," said Fei with a frown.

Penelope broke the silence that followed.

"Why did he stop?" asked Penelope.

Yamashita looked up at her. "That's an excellent question. Why indeed..."

Penny stood up and went to draw the curtains.

"I think it's *the* question," she said. "This person stopped, most likely because they had killed whomever they wanted to kill. And maybe they will stop again when they kill someone they want to kill."

They all looked at her silently, and then Fei shook her head. "Or they got sick, or they went to prison, or they had kids, or they were not in the country...."

"Or some of these murders were real, and others were distractions…" smiled Penelope.

Sal and Yamashita looked at each other with raised eyebrows.

"Then why not kill totally random people then, and not people connected to *shogi* or the case?" asked Yamashita.

Penelope sat down and folded her arms, and stared at Yamashita.

"Because making you assume there *is* a connection between *all* of the victims is more confusing for you," she said flatly. "This person is all about deception and red herrings and leading you up the garden path. It's all planned, that's what I think. None of this is random. Every victim is carefully selected for a specific purpose. Hence, that's why the reason this person stopped the last time is the big question. And it's very, *very* related to why they started again. Find the answer to *that*, and it will lead you directly to them."

"Wow… Penny…" said Fei. "You are out on a limb there."

Sal smiled at them all.

"I think she's right," he said. "I think that's exactly how you catch them."

Penelope smiled. "Well, thank you, Sal, at least one person has faith in me. Here is a question, however. Let's go back to the first murders eighteen years ago…"

"OK," said Yamashita. "What do you want to talk about?"

"Was there a letter before the first killing? The one of Terumoto's wife?"

"No," said Sal. "No letter."

"So the letters started with the second killing. The Enamotos, who were the neighbors?"

"Yes, that's right," nodded Yamashita.

"OK, then. Let's assume Terumoto killed his wife, and the current killer did the Enamoto couple. Why kill *them,* though? Why not kill a totally random person? Or just someone you dislike? Remember, this is a *different* killer."

"Well, as we said before, all the killings are connected by *shogi* or by the case."

Penelope nodded. "Yes, but they don't have to be. The chain starts at the second killing, not the first. The killing of the wife, if we assume that's by Terumoto, who presumably has just had enough of her and wants to move on, that's not connected to *shogi* or the case."

"I don't follow you," said Yamashita with a confused look.

"Well, what I am saying is what if the second couple were killed because the killer *wanted* to connect the killing of Terumoto's wife with their death? In other words, he *wanted* to establish a connection between the two killings and thus deliberately implicate himself in the wife's killing."

Sal and Yamashita looked at each other.

"You mean he wanted to tell the world, "Look, I killed all of them. The wife and the Enamoto couple," said Sal.

Penelope nodded. "Why would you want to do that?"

There was silence in the room for a long moment.

"Because it gets Terumoto off the hook?"

Penelope nodded again. "Exactly. And again, why would you want to do that?"

"Because you wanted to protect him?" said Fei.

Penelope smiled.

"Then why go on and kill Watanabe? If you have established that it maybe wasn't Terumoto that killed the wife?"

"Was Terumoto freed after the death of the Enamoto couple?"

"No, that took a bit longer," said Yamashita.

"Maybe that's your answer," said Penelope. "Anyway, it's just a thought."

Yamashita stood up to leave. "I have to be getting back to the station folks. It's been … very illuminating…" he said, and he took his leave thanking Penelope for the meal, as did the others.

Alone in her home with her cats, Penelope made some tea and sat musing on the case until late in the night. In the back of her head, an idea was forming, and the elusive face of the murderer was coming more and more into focus. She had an idea, and it was going to be a long shot, but she thought that Sal particularly might not mind if she could just convince him and find a means of carrying it out.

It was worth a chance though, she thought. First, however, there was someone she had to see.

=====================

The next morning she knocked on Mari's door, and the artist showed her inside.

"So… how is she?" Penelope asked.

Mari nodded towards the garden, where she saw Suzume sitting on a bench with her back turned to them.

121

"She seems to be in shock," said Mari. "I took her to the doctor, but he just said to get some rest and see how things go. I'm beginning to think she may need something more, however. Counselling, or something…."

Mari made them some coffee, and they sat at the large wooden dining table.

"She must have been very close to him to take it this hard…" said Penelope.

Mari nodded. "She was. Apparently, they were in love…."

Penelope gasped. "Really? But she is…."

Mari nodded. "A kid. Maybe twenty years or so younger than him. And his student…." she added, with a frown.

"Wow," said Penelope. "That's not good… how did you find out?"

Mari smiled grimly. "Not in the most, well, orthodox of ways. I went through her phone when she was asleep. There were messages. Not all that many, but I was able to see some that had not been deleted."

Penelope shot a glance at the garden.

"Did you talk to her about it?"

Mari sighed and nodded. "Yeah, she told me eventually. I didn't tell her I went through her phone, so please don't mention that. But when I asked her about it… in the end, she told me the truth. They were planning to marry when she was older."

Mari took a sip of her coffee. "It happens… I don't really blame her. But I do think he was taking advantage of her. I mean, she's eighteen, nearly nineteen… but still a kid. He was like thirty-five or something."

"And you had no idea?"

"None," she shook her head. "None at all. But it does make sense now, some of the things she did. The intensity with which she was studying *shogi*. How she spent every spare minute at the school. I mean, I am her aunt, not her mother. I gave her a pretty free hand as to how she spent her time…."

Penelope nodded. "Poor thing. At least now we know why she acted like that when she found out about it. If we had known, we could have broken the news in a better way, perhaps…."

Mari nodded. "Well, no one knew. They kept it all to themselves. If they went on a date, they were just teacher and student. No one was the wiser. If they wanted to be alone, they went up to Tokyo and met there…."

"I guess they had to be discreet. If anyone at the school had found out…."

Mari folded her arms and looked out at where her niece was sitting quietly with their dog at her feet.

"Yes, that would have been the end of him. Old Okamoto would have fired him for sure. He's pretty straight-laced and old-fashioned, I hear."

"Yes, I'm sure. Did she know about the father?"

Mari shot her a pained look, like it was something she would rather not talk about.

"It was on the news," she said.

"Yes. There has been a bit of discussion about it. That family seems to be cursed," said Penelope.

"Well… I knew about it. It was big talk in the *shogi* world back in the day. I didn't know Yasuo was connected to the school, however. Anyway, I don't want her at the funeral. She's not ready for that yet."

"Yes, I imagine she's not," said Penelope. "Do you want me to talk to her?"

"Sure. It might do her some good. Why not?" said Mari.

"OK. I won't be long."

Penelope stood, walked into the old Japanese garden, and approached the bench where Suzume was sitting quietly. The dog, an old orange Pomeranian, wagged its tail as she approached.

"Hi," she said.

Suzume looked up. Her eyes were puffy, but otherwise she seemed to be calm.

"Hi, Penny-*sensei*," she said quietly.

Penelope sat down on the bench.

"I'm sorry for your loss, Suzume. Your aunt told me that you were very close…."

Suzume nodded sadly and looked at the ground.

"I guess you think I'm foolish. I mean, the age difference and everything…."

Penelope smiled.

"No, not at all. We don't get to choose how we feel about people sometimes. It just happens….."

"Yes," she said. "That's right. It just happened. And now it's over."

They were quiet for a while, and Penelope let her talk. She told her about how they had studied together and how they had grown close that way. He had been single and lonely, she said. And they had been good together, she maintained. They were a normal couple in many ways; after all, many women married men older than them. They had always had a special connection, she felt, like they were cut from the same cloth, the same type of people.

124

She went on for a while, telling Penelope everything, like a dam had burst inside her.

In the end, she fell silent and started to sob.

Penelope put her arm around her shoulders. "You know, let me ask you something. *Shogi*. Was that your dream? Or were you interested in becoming a pro because of Yasuo-san? I mean, was he the real motivation for you?"

Suzume shook her head.

"No. It was my dream. It was his dream for me, too. He wanted me to become a professional...."

Penelope smiled at her and took both her hands in hers.

"Then, you know what you have to do then. You have to get back to work, and make both your dreams come true. What do you think? Is that a plan?"

Suzume looked up at her.

"Yes. You're right," she nodded.

"I know I am. The same thing happened to me once, long ago. Work is sometimes the best medicine."

Penelope stood and made her way back to the kitchen.

"How did it go?" asked Mari.

Penelope brushed a tear from her eye.

"She's going to be OK," she said.

Chapter 11

A Game of War

It was a somber-looking Thursday morning that day, with dark clouds gathering over the western hills and the old stone steps leading up to the ancient temple slick and shining dully underfoot. As she entered the massive wooden gates, she heard a train behind her on the little track that stood just a few meters away and turned and watched it for a moment.

Engakujii was one of the oldest Zen temples in Japan, founded by the great Dogen Zenji in the early fourteenth century after his return from studying Buddhism for many years in China. It was rumored that the famous monk had been the illegitimate child of an emperor, but even if that were true, he had turned from the court and devoted himself to one thing and one thing only, the attainment of enlightenment.

And that was why he had founded this temple.

Penelope had been coming here every Thursday morning for more than twenty years for a *zazen* meditation class conducted in English, a language she hardly used these days except with Fei and a few other Japanese friends occasionally, who also spoke it extremely well.

One of the other reasons she came was also to see Dokan, who was Chief Inspector Yamashita's older brother, apart from being the head monk and future abbot of the monastery. Dokan had often taught the class himself as he was a fluent English speaker, but these days he was too busy running things in the monastery, so he usually delegated the task to one of the other monks or lay people.

Engakuji regarded the class as their way of helping Zen reach the outside world, and many foreigners came here to attend when they were in Kamakura, which was famous as the home of Zen Buddhism in Japan and still possessed some of the oldest and most outstanding temples of both the main Rinzai and Soto Zen schools.

That day, maybe because of the weather, there were few people at the class except for the regulars, so after the meditation and the dhamma talk, which lasted about an hour, she sought out Dokan in his office at the back of the complex near the monk's quarters.

"Ah, Penny-*sensei*! I was wondering if I would see you today. I hear you have been busy with my brother again."

Penny sat down on the cushion he offered her in front of his low desk. The little office was small but beautifully organized, without a speck of dust anywhere.

"Would you like some tea?" asked Dokan, placing a small cup in front of her.

"Yes, please. I don't know if busy really describes it, I know your brother has been working very hard, however."

"Yes, I read about it in the papers. I think I saw it on television too. The *shogi* killings. Do you think the killer has really returned after all these years?"

Penny sipped her tea, the usual strong green tea the monks drank here to keep them awake during meditation. The news about the killings had been all over the TV recently, as this kind of thing in Japan was incredibly rare, and the killing of a police officer like Toyozaki had been big news. Nevertheless, she was surprised a monk like Dokan knew about it, but then he seemed to have quite a good idea as to what was going on in the outside world, unlike many of his brother monks, who deliberately isolated themselves from the affairs of the world. She had once met one elderly monk in another monastery who had no idea who was the American president, and another friend of his that had been surprised to hear that Ronald Reagan was still not in office.

"It would appear so. There's been two killings now."

"And four the last time, I believe, all those years ago. Do you think it's going to continue? Or stop again?"

She shook her head. "There's no way to know, I'm afraid. I was wondering the same thing. I mean, last time there were four, and then it stopped. But who knows?"

Dokan smiled and scratched his bald pate.

"Now, what makes you say that? I wonder…"

Penny smiled too. Dokan was always teasing her to get her opinion on things.

"I have no idea. Simply that the last time this happened, it stopped for no reason at four killings, like the killer had achieved whatever goal they had, and so I'm naturally wondering if this time it will be the same."

"So you don't think it's just random?"

"No, I don't. Absolutely not."

"And what do you think the purpose of all this is?"

128

Penelope sighed. "That's what I am trying to figure out. I think a single thread connects the two sets of crimes. But... apart from the fact they're not random, I have no idea what that might be."

Dokan sat back on his cushion and poured some tea into the usual chipped old tea cup he always used.

"Well, it's nice to see you are sure of one thing. My brother and the police seem to be sure of nothing at all."

Penny sighed and played with the chain of her necklace. "I'm sure there's a pattern. I just can't see it. That's the problem."

"Well, never mind. I know you. I'm sure it'll come to you in time. *Shogi* and chess are strange games. Beautiful games too... and often unusual people are the most attracted to them."

"I didn't know you were a fan," she said. "I've never been able to get my head around either of them."

Dokan nodded. "I understand. They appeal to some people and not to others. I guess it's how your brain is wired. I used to play chess, you know, Western chess, when I was at school. I got quite into it. Maybe it was because my brother was so fascinated by *shogi*, I don't know. They are equally games of war, both on the board and between the opponents. Of course, *shogi* is way more complicated, because if you lose a piece it can be returned to the board and used by your opponent. That increases the number of possible moves exponentially. But chess is still beautiful too, and I understand people's attraction to it."

"I guess there's that. Why don't you play now? Your brother's still into *shogi*."

Dokan sipped his tea.

"Yes, he is, isn't he? I think it's a refuge for him, from his work. Maybe from other things too. These games… they're all so absorbing. They take you completely out of your life and put you in another world, a world of strategy, planning and calculation," he smiled. "I just happen to think that there are more important things to do with the mind. And I have other refuges," he said.

Penelope smiled. "Like not thinking at all."

Dokan nodded. "Exactly. That completely changes your life, as you probably know. I'm not sure games do that. I don't see the benefit, other than that they amuse… Maybe they're just something else to do with your time before you die."

Penelope felt a shiver run through her. Coming to this place and listening to him always made her aware that whatever time she had left was shorter than she imagined. What was she doing with her time?

She stared at the large pile of old-looking books on Dokan's desk.

"What are they? Are you cleaning up?" she asked.

Dokan tapped on the cover of the top book.

"These… I don't know who started these, and I don't know why I suddenly got the urge to look at them, but they have been gathering dust here for years…" he passed her one of the books.

Inside there was page after page of black and white pictures, mostly of monks going about their daily lives in the monastery, cooking, cleaning, meditating, repairing various things, building other things outside, and working in the monastery gardens.

Dokan sighed, "Some of these books date back to the 1950s, believe it or not. There are tons more of them in storage too. I just got a few of them out recently to see what kind of condition they are in. You wouldn't believe the amount of stuff we have in some of the old warehouses. A lot of it ought to be in museums, not rotting here."

Penelope nodded. Monasteries often had huge repositories of very important historical material that no one ever saw from one generation to the next, and she and other academics were always trying to find out what exactly they were holding. People had often used them in the past as places where important treasures could be stored in troubled times, and then things had just got left there more or less permanently.

Monasteries could also be very weird about who they gave access to, and some places even had rooms they only allowed people into just once every century or so. In one very recent instance, a page from a ninth-century copy of *The Tale of Genji,* hand-written by the famous Heian Period courtier Teika Fujiwara, had turned up in a similar monastery after it hadn't been seen for over a hundred years. It's existence had been recorded, and then forgotten about until a visiting researcher stumbled across it when they were looking for something else.

That's just the way monasteries were.

Penelope leafed through the book. "These are very interesting," she said. "It's nice you have a photographic record of life here. Do you know some of these people?"

Dokan laughed. "Oh yes, some of them. The more recent ones, anyway. Some of the people in these books are still here and very old they are too. Many have left or died or gone to other monasteries, though," he said, pointing to one figure in blue workman's clothes working in the steamy kitchen.

"I remember *him* very well. His name was Soju. He was my old meditation master when I was young and was in charge of all the novices. A very kind man, he later became abbot and died… a long time ago now. I think he was here almost his entire life."

"Like you?"

"Me? I've only been here thirty years. That's nothing in the Zen world."

"Well, it's something for me. I've been coming here for a while too. I think I started about twenty years ago myself." She placed her teacup on his desk and passed him back the book. "Anyway, I just popped in to say hello. I'll let you get back to your work."

"OK. Come and say hello again next time you are here. Or ask my esteemed brother to arrange another of his soirees at the house, and I will pop in and we can cook together again. Do give my regards to Fei-san, too."

"I will. It's been a while since we got together there. The maple trees will be looking nice soon," she said wistfully.

Chief Inspector Yamashita's home was very close by, near the neighboring Meigetsu-in temple, and they all occasionally had dinner together, where Penelope and Dokan did the cooking. It was an old wooden house in the Western style they had inherited from their parents, who had retired there, and the gardens were lovely, especially in the spring and autumn.

Penelope left him to his work, and walked down the long path again through the ancient temple to the main gate. The temple was in the north-eastern part of Kamakura and hard by the little Kita-Kamakura station, from where you could be in the center of the town in just a few minutes. As she approached the railroad tracks, she decided on a whim to visit an old bookstore she knew in the main shopping street, so she caught the train back the big Kamakura station from where it was a short walk.

It was fairly quiet as she walked along past all the familiar shops to the old second-hand bookstore, where she was hoping, as she often did, to track down a book of poetry by an old Edo-period author that had long gone out of print. Fortunately, the shop was just opening as she arrived, and she was given a cordial greeting by the owner, who knew her well.

The tumbledown old bookshop was run by the parents of one of her old students at Hassei university where she had taught for so many years, and had been in the family for a long time before that. Its strong point was that it had a lot of old literary books and poetry, and she had often come across various treasures there that she had assumed were impossible to find anymore.

The only problem with the bookshop, which was named simply 'Mitsunari,' which was the family name, was that it was hopelessly disorganized. This seems to be a feature of many second-hand bookshops across the globe, as if it is some kind of treasure hunt organized by the owners who don't want to make it too easy for anyone to find something they want without first digging through piles of unrelated items first.

The Mitsunari bookshop, which was extremely well known among the Kamakura locals, was no exception to this rule, and enjoyed teetering piles of odd books piled from floor to ceiling and on large tables, as well as all over the walls and climbing up the rickety staircase in small piles to the second floor, which, if anything, was worse.

If you were after a particular book, the owners had absolutely no idea where it was. If you asked them this stupid question, they simply shrugged and waved in the direction of the books as if to say, 'help yourself." And so, nobody asked.

Fortified with a large cappuccino from the cafe next door, Penelope opened the door and headed to the second floor, where for some unknown reason she had seen more books on poetry than in the stacks downstairs, and began to rummage through the shelves and tables, which were groaning with books of all sorts, none of which had been dusted in centuries.

Midway through this endeavour, and having stopped several times to sneeze violently, she stumbled upon the very book she was looking for. With a small cry of exaltation, she sat down on the floor to thumb through her prize, for which she had been looking for a number of years.

As she sat there, happy with her discovery, her eye happened to fall upon a stack of old magazines next to her that were piled up in an old cardboard box.

She took out the top one, which had the faded title of *Shogi Today*. It appeared to be a vintage magazine from the 1980s, and had a lot of information and pictures of *shogi* matches and various tournaments, including local ones from around the Tokyo region.

She pulled the rest of the magazines from the box and discovered around fifty or so periodicals covering a range of about twenty years, from the 1980s until the early 2000s. Someone had obviously been devotedly collecting them, and, maybe finding no further use for them, had brought them here and sold them, probably for very little.

On a whim, she started to go through all the magazines from the 2000s backward, looking mainly at the pictures which were all subtitled with the player's names, wondering if she could find any mention of the Terumoto school, or even Terumoto himself, in them.

After looking through about five magazines, she found what she was looking for.

There he was, standing next to a group of young people, one of whom was holding a small silver cup. Everyone was smiling and happy, as they had clearly just won some tournament or other. What struck her most of all though was the astonishing resemblance of the young Terumoto to his recently deceased son, Yasuo. They had the same muscular build, the same open, handsome face, and deep romantic eyes.

How changed he was now, she thought, thinking back to the man she had observed sitting just a few meters from her in the *shogi* parlor, his face thin and creased with age and worry, and his whole demeanor seemingly sunk in a quagmire of depression. She wondered if he knew what had happened to his son, and how that had affected him. It must have been just another devastating blow in a lifetime of pain.

She put all the magazines back in the box and then, cursing herself for being completely stupid, took them downstairs and, in addition to her long sought-after book, bought the whole box of *Shogi Today*, no doubt much to the delight of the Mitsunari household.

As she lugged the box out onto the street outside, she wondered if she would have even started looking for the photo of Terumoto at all if she had not first seen the books on Dokan's desk back at Engakuji. Something about the way old photographs allowed you to peer into the past to some degree opened up a way that, however obscure, might offer a chance to grasp what had happened to Terumoto, and maybe a way of being able to find why he had acted as he did or what had happened to him to cause the terrible chain of events that had engulfed his life.

Whether or not Terumoto had killed his wife, the person who had killed all the others must have known him. And if they *had* known him, had it been through *shogi*? That would seem likely. But would they be in these magazines, and could she identify them? That was a completely different question, and one where the odds were stacked hugely against her.

There was only one way to find out.

She took the heavy box back to the train station where she managed to find a taxi, and was soon back at home with her cats, who found the box, as cats always do, much more interesting than its contents.

Chapter 12

Mothers and Daughters

About two weeks after Yasuo's funeral, which both she and Fei had attended along with half of the Japanese media, who had, with their usual complete lack of scruple, camped in their legions outside the funeral parlor, Penelope decided to return Mari's hospitality and invite her and Suzume for dinner. Her thinking was that it also might do Suzume some good to get out of the house and, if possible, play some *shogi* with Fei if she felt up to it.

Mari had accepted her invitation with pleasure but had asked if Suzume's mother, who was visiting from Akita, could also come along, an idea Penelope had accepted.

Suzume, who as it turned out was obsessed with cats, had been delighted when she was greeted at the door by no less than all four of Penelope's felines, who regarded door duty as their sacred right and insisted on vetting any new person that entered the house.

"Oh, I didn't know you had all of these guys!" said Suzume, picking up the first cat she saw, a huge old white and orange stray that Penelope had rescued as a kitten many years ago, like all the rest of her cats. Biscuit, as he was named, was a particularly affectionate old tomcat and purred happily in her arms, and then proceeded to follow her around the house for the rest of the evening.

"Ah, he likes you," said Penelope. "He doesn't go to everyone."

Suzume smiled happily and scratched the cat behind his ears.

"That's right," said Fei, appearing from the kitchen to greet the guests. "The little hound doesn't even come to me, and I'm here all the time!"

Suzume's mother appeared last in the doorway, and Mari introduced her.

"This is my sister Junko," she said.

Junko bowed. She was a plump middle-aged woman with shoulder-length greying hair and a reassuringly down-to-earth country manner that endeared her to Penelope. Unlike Mari, who was quite a bit younger and much more fashionable looking, she was comfortably dressed in beige slacks and a cardigan, wore no makeup, and generally made absolutely no attempt to look other than she was.

Looking at the mother and daughter standing next to each other, Penelope found it hard to see a family resemblance. Still, there was something about the eyes of the three women that bespoke some kind of relationship. If anything, Suzume looked far more like her aunt, who also had a slim figure and wore her hair past her shoulders, like her niece.

For dinner that night, Penelope had broken into her supplies of a particularly good chablis she often bought by the case when she had the money, and decided to serve her guests a meal from her French repertoire, starting with a cold vichyssoise soup and followed by a hearty boeuf bourguignon and herb bread, a recipe she had got from her maternal grandmother, who had been French and also from Burgundy where the dish had originated.

"That smells wonderful, Penny-*sensei*," said Mari as she took a seat in the living room.

"It does," agreed her sister. "What is it?"

Penelope smiled and explained. "It's basically a French beef stew. Very simple. It just needs a few hours in a slow cooker to get right."

"Wow..." said Junko as Penelope lifted the top off the pot to show her the dish. "It looks like the real deal. What a wonderful aroma...." She waved her hand over it to beckon the smell towards her.

"Don't try it. It took like about eight hours. She's been at it since this morning," remarked Fei, who had helped her chop up the vegetables but then deserted her in favor of reading her beloved Asahi newspaper for the rest of the morning.

Junko looked out on the vegetable garden, which was only just visible in the gathering dusk.

"Ah... this reminds me of home. We have a large garden ourselves. My uncle does all the work, however. What do you grow here?"

Penelope took her out on the little wooden verandah to see better.

"Well, it depends on the season. All the usual summer vegetables," she pointed to the various beds and pots. "Lots of eggplants, tomatoes, and cucumbers, quite a lot of potatoes, butternut squash, other pumpkins, some melons. This is a passionfruit vine, of course. Japanese radish, Chinese cabbage, edamame and other beans, lots of herbs... just about everything. I hardly ever buy vegetables, especially in the warmer months. We can do just about everything here. And it feeds Fei and her aunt as well. They live next door there," she said, pointing at the neighbouring house. "Soon, we will be doing the pickles for the winter…" she smiled.

"*Tsukemono*… that's very Japanese," Junko remarked admiringly. "We do a lot of pickles too, where I'm from, up in the snow country. And you use these?" she pointed to a row of large ceramic jars on the other end of the balcony.

Penelope nodded. "Yes, I got those in the Kiso valley in Nagano some years ago. We always do our pickling in those. I think they taste better…" she explained.

Junko asked many questions about how they grew things here and the climate and soil and generally displayed a farmer's in-depth knowledge about all agricultural matters.

They went back inside, and Fei poured them a glass of wine while Suzume acquainted herself with Alphonse, Marmalade and Coco, the other three cats who now surrounded her and took turns fighting for a place on her lap.

"So you said your uncle does the gardening? Do you have a lot of family near you?" asked Penelope.

Junko shook her head. "Not too many now. We share a house with my uncle and aunt, who are quite elderly now. My husband passed away before Suzume was born."

"Oh, I'm sorry to hear that," said Penelope. "That must have been hard."

Junko smiled. "Well, at the time. But then Suzume came along, so that was enough. We were married about ten years, and we had a lot of problems having children. It was kind of a gift. In the end," she looked at her sister, who reached

140

over and held her hand affectionately, which Penelope found a slightly uncharacteristic gesture for Japanese.

Fei helped serve the food and Penelope then had to field a lot of questions from Junko about the recipes she had used. It was the first time she had eaten either of the dishes, and she enjoyed them enormously.

"Up in Akita, we don't go out that much to restaurants, and if we do it's always Japanese. Auntie and uncle are old, and they won't eat anything else. So this is a real treat for me. I want to start eating more Western food occasionally... even if ..."

Fei smiled. "Even if it's bad for you. I know. To tell the truth, I only eat Japanese food if I go out for *yakitori* with Penny. I also live with my aunt, and she does all the cooking. She believes Japanese food is some kind of deadly poison. And when I come over here, Penny only cooks Western food. So I sometimes wonder if I live in Japan at all...."

"Well, you are welcome to take over the kitchen and cook Japanese food here anytime, you know... Except, I have never seen you cook anything, other than pot noodles..." laughed Penelope.

"Hmmm... I have other skills," said Fei. "And I am about to demonstrate them." She looked at Suzume, who had just finished her meal.

"OK, young lady. I have something for you. You want to see it?" she asked.

Suzume smiled. "Really? Sure!"

Fei cleared a space between her and Suzume and then presented her with a large and very heavy cardboard box.

"You could have at least wrapped it, Fei," said Penelope reprovingly.

Fei waved her away, and Suzume opened the box and took out a beautiful *shogi* board, which she placed carefully in front of her. Even at a glance, the board looked very old and quite unlike the modern ones that Penelope was more used to seeing.

"Oh my god, Fei-san…" she said, and tears welled up in her eyes.

Mari also seemed to recognize the value of the board immediately.

"Oh… Fei. That's too much…" she whispered.

Fei shrugged and smiled.

"This was given to me a long time ago by my teacher, Watanabe-*sensei*. It had been in his family for generations, and to tell the truth, I have a collection of antique boards, so I don't use this. I haven't used it for years, so it was just gathering dust. Suzume should have it."

She tapped the old board with her fingers.

"This is *kaya* wood. It's banned now, but this board is over two hundred years old. *Kaya* is still the best wood for *shogi* and *igo* boards. You can see the beautiful dark gold grain it has, and also the sound…."

She passed a *shogi* piece to Suzume, who took it and slapped it in the traditional manner on the board with a sharp clicking sound.

"Beautiful," she said, brushing away a tear.

"The lines on the board," continued Fei "are cut with a *katana,* a Japanese sword. Such things take a lot of skill, and you never see boards like these today, unfortunately. Anyway, as I said, I have others like this. So, this is for you, Suzume. After all, you're the future."

Suzume burst into tears at this point and got out of her seat and hugged Fei. The other women also felt about to cry.

"OK, let's have some more wine… and then you can give me a game on your new board. OK?" said Fei, standing up and brushing away a tear herself.

Penelope served them dessert while Suzume set up the pieces on the *shogi* board for their game. She seemed much happier and more at peace than the last time they had talked a few weeks before, and Penelope thought she looked like she was beginning to get over the shock of losing Yasuo in such a sudden and dreadful way. She was also proud of Fei, who had offered to give her such a meaningful gift without a second thought, even though it was something she had been given by her late teacher, whose memory Penelope knew she treasured, even if Fei would never have admitted it.

"Was your husband a *shogi* player, Junko-san? I was asking Mari-san before where she got her flair for the game."

Junko looked a bit shocked at the question. "Oh… no. I don't think I ever saw him play any game. He was a farmer, like the rest of his family. No… she must get it from her aunt…" she said proudly, looking at Mari, whom she clearly admired, even though she was the younger sister.

Mari looked up and frowned. "Me? I doubt it. That was years ago, anyway. I haven't touched a *shogi* board in like,… forever. Too busy with paintings I'm afraid…."

"Oh… but you used to play?" asked Fei, looking up.

Mari waved her away. "Yeah, but I've forgotten everything. I dunno if I even remember the names of the pieces these days. Can I help you with the dishes, Penelope?"

she said, changing the subject in a tone that indicated she didn't want to talk about it.

Penelope took the hint, and they started to clear the table, to the sound of *shogi* pieces clicking on the old wooden board from the two players at the other end. Mari and Junko came into the kitchen to help her, and for a moment they could talk without being overheard by Suzume.

"How is she getting along?" asked Penelope.

Mari shrugged. "It's hard to tell. Some days are better than others. But seeing you the other week definitely seemed to help lift her spirits. Getting her to think about something else, like her *shogi* ambitions, is probably the best medicine."

Junko nodded. "Yes, I agree. She needs to concentrate on something else."

"It might also be good for her to find a different trainer in another school. Fei can probably help with that, she knows a lot of people in the *shogi* world. She definitely should not go back to her old school I think, there are just way too many memories of Yasuo-san there."

Junko and Mari agreed.

"I met him once... Yasuo-san," said Junko sadly. "He seemed like such a nice person."

Mari looked at the floor and said nothing, but Penelope could sense she strongly disagreed with what her sister was saying.

"You didn't like him, Mari-san?" asked Penelope.

Mari sighed.

"No, I did not. I thought he was far too old for her and just taking advantage. Personally, it's a good thing for her that he is out of the picture. The Terumoto family... completely cursed in my opinion..." she said tersely.

Penelope looked a Junko, who appeared shocked but said nothing. Mari was obviously the one in charge of their relationship, and it was clear that Junko was somehow afraid of her sister.

"I wonder how their game is going?" asked Penelope, "Fei said Suzume almost killed her in the last one."

She saw Mari and Junko exchange a look at this remark, but decided it was wisest to let sleeping dogs lie.

===================

That evening, while the women were happily having dinner together, Sal was in his old house just a few miles away, poring over the pile of old magazines that he had gotten from Penelope a few days before.

Sal was a man quite entrenched in his bachelor ways, at least so he thought, and lived mainly on his own when his younger sister was not in town or was between boyfriends, the first being very frequently and the second being exceedingly rare.

As far as his own love life was concerned these days, while there had been women in his life before, his romantic associations never seemed to have much of a shelf-life, and he had been labelled by several of them, rightly or wrongly, as commitment-phobic. Whether this was true was harder to determine than it seemed, but probably the reality was that he simply found his work or whatever he was occupied with at the time more compelling than seeking other company, and they tended not to respond well to this often unintentional neglect.

Not that it mattered much to him. He was pretty happy on his own with his elderly cats and his old black labrador, Algie, for company and with whatever project he was currently investigating for some book or article he was writing.

He was fortunate that now, after many years as a stringer for various newspapers and weekly magazines, he was more able to pick and choose which jobs he did, and there was steady demand from both his publisher and the media for his work, which tended to cater to the darker side of the Japanese public's reading tastes.

He tended not to let things drop, either. Even though he had long since published his work on several famous criminal cases, mainly involving money, politics, fraud and various unsolved mysteries such as the present case, he always kept an open interest in them, and the *Shogi* Ripper, which had been the subject of his first and most successful book, had always been one of them.

Sometimes things took time, and Sal was a patient man. Despite absolutely nothing coming to light to further the investigation into this case either from his side or from the efforts of the police for many, many years now, he had still kept tabs on the elder Terumoto, and spent a great deal of time just thinking and going over his old notes, until suddenly, years later, the case had exploded back into life again.

Sal had a hunger in his heart for the truth, a desire that he knew had always been there but which he had never been able to satisfy.

Was this going to be the chance to solve it finally? Somehow, he doubted it. Whomever the killer was, they were just too careful, no matter how brazen the killing. He found this particularly true in the killing of Yasuo, in broad daylight with a hundred people just next door and with the possibility of being seen or caught just seconds away at any time.

Either that showed nerves of steel, or else maybe the killer just wanted to be caught for some reason. That kind of thing happened, he knew.

It was these things that drove him now in his lonely quest for the truth, and had made him one of the doyens of investigative journalism in Japan. If anyone had asked him what it took to be good at his kind of work, he had a simple answer. Stay curious. Be patient. Wait.

That was how you caught people, and that was why he was sitting at his desk now past midnight with just his lonely old lamp burning, having forgotten to eat, and with a cold cup of coffee and Algie snoring peacefully in his basket as the hours ticked by.

The box full of the ancient, tattered copies of *Shogi Today,* which he had picked up at Penelope's urging a few days before, had given him an idea, but it was not a very clear one, and he was unsure exactly what it was that he was really looking for.

Penelope's idea that the killer knew Terumoto through *shogi* had merit, and he acknowledged that. It was perhaps the least tenuous of all the many theories he and others had entertained in the past, and as such, it deserved some time from him. What else did he or the police have anyway?

As he leafed carefully through the old magazine with its grainy black and white photographs, he had begun to mark all the pictures of Terumoto that he found, both father and son. But now he began to wonder who the other people in the photographs were. Were they any relation to Terumoto in the period before his wife died?

Sighing, he went back to the first magazine. He began to list anyone in the magazine associated with Terumoto or his school, including anyone that had played against Terumoto in the five years before his wife died. And before long, his list started to grow.

It was a long and tedious job, but after several hours, he had a list of names. Some of these, mainly the prominent players, he knew. The rest was simply a long list of others who had appeared with Terumoto in photographs and people who were listed as his students or opponents or who had some other connection. These he did not know.

As dawn broke, he sat back, stretched, and tapped his pen on his pad.

The point which had begun to bother him more than anything else was that *Shogi Today* was only one source of information. There were bound to be others. Other magazines. Other people.

He needed to track them down. All of them. But where to begin?

He turned on his laptop and began to make another list of all the shops in Tokyo and Kamakura that sold *shogi* equipment and books. Surely, he thought, one of these guys would know where he should look next and could perhaps point him in the right direction.

The whole thing might be a dead end. But something in the back of his mind was telling him that, at long last, he was on to something.

Chapter 13

The Last Opponent.

The phone call, which came just before lunch the following day, caught Sal completely by surprise.

He had been asleep on his sofa after spending the entire night going through the magazines, and it took him a while to stagger to his feet and answer it.

It was a short call, but after he had hung up, he stood there staring at the phone for the next several minutes trying to decide what to do.

It came to him that in all the years he had been researching and writing about the Ripper case, he had never heard the chief suspect's voice before, and his gentle tone and manner of speaking had so surprised him that at first, he had doubted if it was even the person the caller claimed to be.

Terumoto had never said even a single word to anyone after his acquittal all those many years before. Yet here he was on the other end of the line, wanting to talk to Sal. He had been pursued relentlessly by the media to give his views on the case, especially after the dramatic acquittal, and offered large sums of money to give interviews and appear on television, but he had refused all advances and had maintained a total silence about the whole affair.

Sal had wondered at the time if Terumoto's stony silence had been an indication of his guilt or otherwise, but in the end, he had come to feel that the response was more that of an individual whose life had been extinguished by his persecutors and who did not want to give them the satisfaction of gaining any further advantage from him.

During his call this morning, Terumoto had been brief and to the point.

"I have something to say to you that I know you will be interested in. I know you have been following me for years, and I even saw you at my club recently. If you want to learn the truth about these murders, come to my house at 7 p.m. tonight. I know you already have the address, I've seen you parked outside often enough. That's all I have to say now. Will I expect you?" he asked.

Sal stood stunned for a long moment.

"OK. I'll be there."

"Good. You can bring your lady friend if you like. Yes, I know who she is. I will leave that up to you, though."

And with those final words, the line had gone dead.

Finally, Sal slumped into his chair to think.

Eighteen years of silence, and now this? A phone call out of the blue to a man he probably hated, a man who had written a book that had placed the blame for his wife's murder squarely on him, a murder he had been fully acquitted of committing. And from a man who had not said one word, not one, either during his trial or after it?

The word 'shocked' did not even begin to cover the feelings that raced through his mind at that moment.

He pulled himself together and headed for the shower to clear his head, and then he called Penelope.

A few hours later, he arrived at her house, and as always she made him tea and sat down to hear what he had to say. Penelope had been expecting him to talk about the magazines she had given him to inspect, something she knew he had been eager to do, but this news was entirely unexpected.

Sal carefully explained everything that Terumoto had told him, including his invitation for her to come along.

"Of course, I'll come. I wouldn't miss it for the world," said Penelope instantly. "There are many things I want to ask that man. I'm sure you have a few questions too…What did he sound like? I'm very curious to meet him."

"He sounded… I dunno. Kind of beaten up. Quiet. Like he just wanted to get things over with finally," Sal sipped his coffee. "But you bet, I have a lot of questions. Mainly I just want to know finally whether or not he is prepared to own up to his wife's murder after all these years. That's the most important thing, I think."

Penelope nodded.

"Well, you might want to know that, I know. I have other questions. But first of all, why do you think he has suddenly decided to talk after all these years? Is that to do with him losing his son? Isn't that a bit out of character, at least from what I know of the man from your book?"

"Absolutely it is. He's been as silent as the grave. I really can't believe it," said Sal. "His silence has been quite remarkable. Very few people have the strength to face months of questioning at the hands of the police and then go to trial without speaking. It's quite fascinating. It's one of the things that drew me to this case in the first place, in fact."

Penelope stared into her coffee cup.

"Almost like he was protecting someone, don't you think? That's the only reason I can think of as to how someone could withstand that sort of pressure."

"Possibly, or else he knew that if he could stay silent, it was his best hope of getting off. That's my view on the matter anyway, and what I wrote in the book. I think he always knew that even if the police didn't buy the ridiculous alibi he manufactured when he killed his wife and arrested him, that it would be a different matter when he went to trial, because a judge would have to give him the benefit of the doubt," said Sal.

"Except the judge didn't. He went to jail."

"Briefly. But he always knew he had a chance to win if it went to a court of appeal. He's a clever guy, remember. He wasn't a leading *shogi* player for nothing. This guy thinks ahead, way ahead, and he plans things down to the last detail. That's why I really liked him for the killing of his wife. I would like him for the killing of the others too, because that also shows a very similar level of planning. Except, of course… we can't pin those on him. At least not yet."

"True. But before we run over there to talk to him, there is one more thing…."

"What's that?" asked Sal.

"Well, shouldn't we tell Yamashita-san? I think he should know what's going on. It's his case, and this is potentially a pretty big development…."

Sal looked down and the floor and was silent for a moment.

"Yeah, I have been wondering about that myself. But if the guy has asked to speak to *us,* he may not take kindly to our bringing along the police. Or even discussing it with them. He might just clam up completely again."

"That's true. Nevertheless, I wouldn't feel right not telling him. He trusts me, and we have been friends forever... I don't know if I can really keep this kind of thing from him...."

Sal took out his tobacco and rolled himself a cigarette.

"OK, I understand. We'll tell him then. But he has to let us go and see him as arranged. Like Terumoto wants. After that, he can do what he likes. What do you say?"

Sal looked every inch the reporter he was.

Penelope nodded. "Deal."

=====================

An hour later, Yamashita-san slapped his hand down on Penelope's kitchen table so hard that the plates rattled.

"Let me be crystal clear to both of you. There is absolutely *no way* I am going to let you walk into that man's house without some form of protection. What are you thinking, Sal? This guy is a convicted murderer," scowled Yamashita, who had arrived an hour later and had sat non-plussed at Sal's news.

"Acquitted murderer," corrected Penelope.

"Whatever, he was never acquitted by me," said Yamashita, who, being a policeman to his bones had an entirely negative view of anyone who had set foot inside a

154

prison. "You guys should let the police talk to him if he has anything to say."

Sal offered him the plate of biscuits which he waved away.

"Yeah, but that's the problem. He wants to talk to *us,* not you. If he had wanted to talk to you, he could have bowled down to the police station anytime in the last eighteen years," he said.

The chief inspector frowned into his coffee and sighed.

"I don't like this, Sal. And I wouldn't say I like the idea of you dragging Penny-*sensei* into this. What if the guy wants to make a final statement by killing both of you?"

"I did think of that," said Sal nonchalantly.

The three of them were silent for a while.

"OK, here's the deal," said Yamashita. "You wear a wire. And the S.W.A.T. team and I will wait around the corner. We will give you a safe word. If he even blinks, I will be in there. Do you understand?"

"A wire… hmmm…" mused Sal. "I dunno…"

"For your safety. And particularly for hers…" said Yamashita, nodding at Penelope.

Sal sighed. "OK. Let's do it then. But nothing obvious OK? He's not an idiot."

Yamashita smiled and clapped him on the shoulder. "Don't worry. We have some pretty good tech these days. He won't know about it."

At 6.30 p.m. that evening, a half hour before their appointment with Terumoto, Sal found himself sitting in the back of a large black van that the S.W.A.T. team had parked discreetly in a disused supermarket car park a mile or so from Terumoto's house being wired up by the surveillance technicians, while Penelope waited in the back seat of Yamashita's unmarked car.

The technician, a thin, balding man with no-nonsense metal-rimmed glasses and an air of zen-like tranquillity, went about his work with excruciating slowness.

"Have you worn one of these before?" he asked Sal as he carefully wiped his glasses and held them up to the light.

Sal nodded. "Yeah, once. Several years ago. This one feels very light, though."

The technician nodded. "Yes, in the old days you used to have this thumping great battery in your pants. Sometimes the thing overheated too and burned you… well, you know where…" he smiled. "Now it's all Bluetooth and tiny little wires. Altogether better, in my opinion. You won't even know you have it on."

Sal buttoned up his shirt.

"Just so long as he doesn't pat me down or anything. If he finds it, I'm toast. Remember that," he said.

"Don't worry. Have faith," said the technician with a grin. "You'll be fine."

Penelope, meanwhile, was getting her final instructions from a nervous Yamashita, who made no bones about how he felt about having 'civilians' doing the job of the police.

"OK, I want you to pay attention, Penny. We are going to set up a command post around the corner from his house and wait there. Now, if you feel you are in *danger, and I mean any, say the word 'police' in a sentence, and we will be* there in a few seconds. *Do you understand?*" said Yamashita in an emphatic tone.

"OK. I've got it. Police," said Penny. "This feels like something out of a movie. I don't think the man has any

156

violent intentions, however. Otherwise, why invite both of us? I think he just wants to get something off his chest. And I think I know what it is."

Yamashita raised his eyebrows. "And what do you think that is?"

Penelope looked at him thoughtfully and clasped her hands together on her lap.

"I think losing his son has triggered something in him. I think he may know something, even the name of the person who did all these killings. He may have been protecting them up till now for some reason. But whatever it is, he definitely knows *something*. Something that we don't. And I want to hear what it is."

Yamashita nodded. "Well, that makes two of us. *But...* you watch your step in there. Sal has been in these situations before in his line of work. You haven't. I want you to get the hell out of there if there is even the slightest sign that the guy has some ulterior motive. Got it?"

"I do, Chief Inspector," she said with a mock salute.

Yamashita rolled his eyes.

At the appointed time, the van with the S.W.A.T. team and the other cars assembled as arranged around the corner from Terumoto's house in the same quiet little suburb of Ikegami, and after some final instructions and checking of the sound equipment, Sal and Penelope began walking towards the house.

"Right," said Sal. "This is it then...."

Like the last time they were there, the streets were dark and there wasn't a soul anywhere to be seen. A cold breeze was blowing some autumn leaves in the gutter, and Penelope put her hands in her coat pockets.

"I don't know about you," she said, "but Ikegami gives me the creeps." Penelope had a fairly low opinion of a lot of places in Tokyo, and far preferred the atmosphere of her adopted hometown.

Sal nodded. "I know what you mean. Give me Kamakura any time."

As they approached the house, they saw a dull yellow light glimmering behind the curtains in the downstairs window.

"Well, at least someone's home," said Sal calmly.

Penelope pushed the button mounted on the old cement wall next to the front gate where there was a little metal nameplate that read 'Terumoto', and they heard a bell chiming softly from inside.

They stood quietly waiting for nearly half a minute in the silent street, but no answer came.

Inside the waiting vehicles around the corner, Yamashita looked at Yokota, his second in command, who shrugged.

Standing outside the front gate, Penelope and Sal also looked questioningly at each other and then rang the bell twice more. Finally, after there was no response again, Sal opened the small black metal gate and walked up to the front door and knocked loudly.

Still no answer came, nor was there any sound from inside.

Sal put his hand on the door handle and tugged it toward him, and the door opened a crack.

"It's open... weird..." he whispered back to her.

With his hand still on the handle, he half opened the door. "Hello!" he said in a clear voice.

Penelope heard his voice ring inside the house as she came forward and stood by his side.

158

"Should we go in?" she asked.

Sal opened the door wide and motioned for her to stay put as he took a step into the entranceway of the house, where a single pair of old boots was lined up neatly facing toward the door.

"Hello!" he cried out again.

Once more, there was no answer.

Sal took off his shoes and walked into the house, and Penelope did likewise, despite his request for her to wait outside.

The door to the living room to the right was open, and Sal walked into the room and called out again.

Penelope peeked around the corner of the door and heard Sal curse loudly.

In front of them was the body of a man face down on the living room rug with one arm stretched out in front of him and a pool of blood around his head. The hair on the back of his head was wet with dark blood, and he clearly bore the marks of a brutal beating.

'Shimatta...' whispered Sal.

He carefully approached the body and put his hand on the man's neck for a few seconds.

"He's cold," he said to Penelope. "Yamashita-san, you better get in here. There is a body...." he said calmly for the benefit of the listening police.

Sal looked at Penelope, who was staring at the body, horrified.

"He's dead. Same as the others, I think. We've been beaten to the punch again, it looks like," he said. "Poor bastard..."

Penelope turned and saw an out of breath Yamashita standing behind her.

"You two wait outside. Let me have a look at things," he said as he ushered them out of the house.

The rest of the police had gathered by this time and were waiting outside the gate.

Yamashita eventually reappeared after a few long minutes.

"You're right… he's dead," he said, looking at Sal and Penelope. "Looks like the same MO. And he's holding a *shogi* piece in his hand.

He gave a long sigh.

"And another thing… there is a letter on the desk by the window which looks familiar…." he turned to the waiting police.

"I've checked the rest of the house, it's clear. Yokota? Get forensics here…. It's going to be another long night…."

Chapter 14

Remains of a Life.

The days that followed were particularly trying for the police, and the media had a field day at finding out about yet another murder where the authorities had seemingly no idea who the perpetrator was. Panic among the easily-alarmed public had begun to set in, spurred on by the relentless variety and news programs on television and the weekly magazines who found in the case of the Ripper a gift that kept on giving. Questions had even been asked of the Justice Minister in parliament. As a result, the pressure on the chief inspector to produce any result had become intense.

Perhaps signaling the level of desperation by the authorities, a few days afterward Penelope and Sal were granted special permission to visit the house a second time by the chief inspector, mainly so that Sal could give a second opinion on the many boxes of files that had been discovered and that the police had been unable to learn anything of value from.

They arrived at the house at around 10 a.m. on a bright autumn day, and Yamashita met them outside and informed the officer on guard what was going on.

Penny regarded her friend carefully and thought he looked tired and even a little haggard.

"Are you OK?" she asked, touching him on the arm.

Yamashita nodded. "It's the job," he said with a slight sigh. "Anyway, I'm glad to see you both. God knows I will take any help I can get at the moment."

Penny nodded sympathetically. "Well, we'll do our best. Sal knows more about it than me, though."

"So, what did you find?" asked Sal as they opened the door.

"Well, come and have a look yourself. From what we could see, most of it looks *shogi* related, it may be a lot of stuff from the past when he ran his own school. I know you and Penny have been looking into that, so I thought you might know more about this than we do," he explained.

They walked into the living room where the police had laid out all the boxes of files on the floor.

"Wow, quite a bit of stuff…" said Sal.

"Yes. We were going to take the whole lot to the station, but you might know more about what is worth looking at and what's not. We've already gone through everything, but it doesn't hurt to have a second opinion. I think a lot of this is irrelevant, but… There are more boxes upstairs, by the way, but it's mainly old *shogi* magazines and things like that," said Yamashita.

"Ah… actually, we *are* interested in those."

"Really?"

Sal nodded. "How long have we got?"

Yamashita shrugged. "I'd say at this point you can take your time. We've come up with nothing at all so far."

"Did you say you found another letter?"

Yamashita nodded and, opening his old leather briefcase passed them both a copy of the most recent letter from the killer.

"This was found on that desk. Rather hard to miss, of course."

He pointed to a neat desk underneath the window facing the road.

The letter was in the usual odd faded black script and had obviously been written with a brush like all the others.

Sal held the letter so that Penny could read it too.

Dear little policemen,

Well, it looks like I've killed another one. This one completes the set started all those years ago. Now all the family are together! And once again, you've been unable to stop me. Why is that, do you think? Isn't your job protecting members of the public?

Sorry I didn't give you any warning this time, but I think you've had far too many chances already.

Anyway, I'm getting bored playing this game with you, so I will make you an offer.

If you can figure out the next person to be getting the gold general, I will stop for a while. Maybe a long while.

Good luck!

CS.

Penny took the letter from Sal's hands and read it again.
"Can I take this?" she asked.
Yamashita nodded. "Yes, but be careful with it, OK?"

Penelope promised she would be. "Thanks, I just want to spend some time with it and have a think. This letter is a little unlike the others. The phraseology is a bit unique."

Yamashita smiled. "Great. Just take care of it, and I will pick it up in a couple of days. Copies of this letter are restricted. Anyway, I will leave you to it. Call me immediately if you come up with anything."

"Don't worry, we will," she said.

Yamashita left them and they heard him discussing things with the officer outside.

Sal sat down on the floor and started examining the first of the boxes that had been laid out. It seemed that this type of work was what he had been born for, and he had been anxiously looking forward to starting once they had received Yamashita's invitation.

While he worked, Penny walked around the room.

There were a number of framed photographs on the wall, nearly all of them old, black and white ones. Some were obviously of Terumoto's parents and family members, and there were also a few with him and his son when he was a child.

Penny shook her head in disbelief when she contemplated the fact that both the father and the son had been killed within a few short weeks of each other by the same deranged killer. It was the stuff of television drama in some ways.

A lot of the older photographs seemed to have been taken somewhere in the countryside, and there an old farmhouse featured in a few of them.

"Do you know where Terumoto's family was from?" she asked Sal.

"Up north somewhere, I think," said Sal without looking up.

"Right. I wonder where…."

"Can't help you there. You might need to have a look at the local government family register. Have a look around, I know many people keep a copy of it somewhere."

In the middle of the wall facing them, Penelope's eyes were also drawn to a large blank space where another picture had clearly hung for a long time, but which was missing now. The gap caught Penelope's attention, as the wallpaper was less faded than the area around it, so she removed a couple of the other frames from the wall and saw similar marks underneath them.

She looked around the room, but there were no other framed pictures anywhere else that could have filled the same gap.

"This may be nothing," she said to Sal. "But what do you think used to be here?" she pointed to the wall.

Sal looked up from what he was doing. "Well, clearly a picture or something. I'll keep a lookout for it."

Penelope stood staring at the wall. "It might just be my imagination, but it seems odd. You see all these pictures… they are all in order," She pointed at all the other pictures on the wall in front of her and on the other walls. "All spaced evenly. And then there is this gap…I'm going to have a look around the rest of the house."

Penelope went into the kitchen, which looked a lot like any other kitchen except it was perhaps a bit more orderly, and then made her way upstairs, where there were two bedrooms.

Penelope walked into what was obviously the murdered man's bedroom and stood looking from the door.

"Well…" she said to herself meditatively, looking around. "You certainly were neat for a bachelor."

On the walls were more framed photographs, mainly of *shogi* matches and tournaments, and many featuring Terumoto at play with others. There were also some group photos of children and young people she presumed were members of his old school.

Penelope went over to the neatly made bed and sat down on the old red quilt that covered it.

On the bedside table were several books. She picked one up and read the title:

Advanced Shogi Puzzles. The other books next to the bed were similar.

"So I guess we know how you fell asleep at night," she whispered.

Next to a small chest of drawers, there was another large bookcase, also filled with *shogi* books and several works on Buddhism.

"Not a single piece of fiction…" she said. "What a practical man you were…."

She went into the next bedroom, which was also extremely tidy and had a desk with a laptop on it. It seemed to be some kind of office.

There were more bookcases, some containing folders with legal documents bearing on his trial, more *shogi* books, and on the wall more pictures. There was also a filing cabinet with some neatly labelled hanging files and folders, most of them related to household items and banking documents.

She inspected the pictures closely, sometimes taking them off the wall and carrying them over to the window to see them more clearly.

By the side of the desk on the floor, and slightly obscured by the long hanging curtains was another framed photograph, and this caught her eye immediately.

It showed a young woman in a white dress, smiling as she placed a piece on a *shogi* board. On the other side of the board was Terumoto, who looked to be in his mid-thirties or so and was exclaiming something with a surprised look on his face and pointing a folding fan toward the piece that the girl had just placed. It was clearly a joyous little moment in their lives, and the photographer had caught it perfectly.

On the back of the frame was the handwritten inscription '#2'.

Penelope stared at this for a while.

"Where is #1, I wonder…" she said to herself.

She took the photo off the wall and went downstairs with it to the room where Sal was working his way through the boxes and the piles of files.

"Found anything?" she asked.

Sal shook his head, stretched, and sat back, reaching for his old canvas bag to find his tobacco.

"Nope. Not a thing. A lot of this stuff is just his old files, bits and pieces of miscellaneous stuff, old bills, legal documents, and mixed in with it there is a lot of old *shogi* stuff. He used to write a column in one of these *shogi* magazines. I found a pile of them over there…" he pointed to a couple of large boxes of magazines. "I want to go through all those magazines, but I am saving them till I get through all the rest of the stuff."

167

Penny went over to the wall and held up the framed photo she had brought from upstairs over the gap between the other photographs.

It was too large by several centimeters.

Sal lit his cigarette while he watched her.

"You think that's it?" he asked. "The missing one?"

Penelope shrugged. "No, it's the wrong size…." She passed him the photograph.

Sal looked at it, confused.

"When was this taken?"

Penelope sat down next to him.

"I'd say around twenty years ago."

"Right… well… it really looks like…."

Penelope nodded. "Yes, it does, doesn't it?"

"Maybe she's a time traveller…" said Sal with a smile.

She took out her phone and carefully photographed it while Sal held it up for her.

"Keep an eye out for any photograph with this mark on it," she said, showing him the inscription on the back of the photograph.

Sal nodded. "No problem."

"I'm going to put this back where I found it. Keep looking," she said encouragingly.

She went back upstairs and put the photograph back next to the desk, and looking carefully at the other pictures on the wall, she managed to find several others with the same mysterious girl in them.

"Hmmm… who are you?" she wondered aloud. "You must be one of the students…."

She opened the laptop and saw a post-it note stuck on the screen with the password, doubtless provided by one of the police cyber technicians who had been through it.

She lit up the screen and looked at the desktop, which had very few files on it.

She opened some of them up, and found nothing inside them. It seemed Terumoto was a deeply analog soul, and perhaps hardly ever used his computer. The police would have already checked out any online activity he had.

Sighing, she closed the lid and went back to looking at the bookcases and even looked at the wardrobes and containers where the man's clothing lay hanging or neatly folded.

"This is what we leave behind us," she thought as she rifled through the clothes. "Just a bunch of stuff which people will one day throw in the trash."

There was something particularly sad about going through the meager personal possessions of a sad old man who had led such a troubled life. Someone who did not have much in the way of money, but had tried to make his house a quiet sanctuary where his memories held pride of place. There were no pictures in the house of anything that had taken place since his arrest for the murder of his wife. It was as if his life had just stopped at that point and nothing had occurred since.

She closed the wardrobe and stood back and stared around the room. Apart from the laptop, there was very little else on the desk besides a row of hardback spiral notebooks which the police had no doubt already examined. She opened the drawers of the desk. The top one was filled with neatly arranged stationary supplies, a box of pens, a box of fountain pen refills, a stapler, erasers, and all the usual things. The next drawer was filled with paper and a third with several blank notebooks.

Penelope, who had been a writer all her life and had published or contributed to dozens of books and articles, paused here.

"Have you been writing something, I wonder?" she said aloud.

To her, these stationary supplies looked like someone who had equipped themselves for some kind of large writing project.

She sat down in the chair and took one of the notebooks from the row in front of her.

On the front page, in an impeccably neat handwriting, were the words:

"Notes - The Quiet Game"

After which, there were pages and pages of bullet point notes which she found very difficult to understand.

She opened the rest of the notebooks and found they were all the same, pages of notes all written in bullet points and sometimes with small cryptic headings.

"You *were* writing something…" she whispered.

Picking up all the notebooks, about eight in all, she took them downstairs to Sal, who was now sitting at the desk going through a huge box of old *shogi* magazines.

He looked up and smiled as she came into the room.

"I didn't realize how prolific the guy was. He wrote a lot of columns over many years for these magazines. There are literally hundreds of them here, mainly game analysis, but nothing about him. But there are a lot of links to other people, and photographs. This is much better even than that box you found in the bookshop. He seems to have been quite the author back in the day."

"There's nothing recent though? Nothing after he was arrested?" asked Penelope.

Sal shook his head. "A lot of these articles he wrote are from after the acquittal, but there are no photographs or anything."

Sal eyed the notebooks in Penelope's hand.

"What's that you've got?"

Penelope passed him the bundle of notebooks that had been sitting on the desk upstairs.

"I found these upstairs in his study?"

Sal opened the top one and started to read.

"The Quiet Game?" he said.

He started to leaf through one of the books, and then the next one.

"I'm not real good at reading Japanese handwritten script like that," Penelope said, "but I would say they are notes for a book."

Sal looked up at her. "I think you're right. They seem to be random thoughts and stuff. And rather philosophical too… I'm not sure what this is. There is a long meditation here about loss, losing things, games. Losing possessions. Materialism. Stuff like that… very odd."

Penelope nodded. "Maybe not so odd. I've plotted some of my own books like that, except I use a laptop. He seems to have been more a pen-and-paper guy. I dunno, but to me that looks like notes for some kind of philosophical manifesto or maybe… an autobiography? Or both? There are dates in there too. And I saw some place names."

"Yeah…" said Sal as he continued to leaf through the other notebooks. "I would say… yeah. This looks like some kind of personal history mixed with a philosophical rant… there are repeated sections here about *shogi* strategy and its relationship to life. He was definitely writing something like that. I would have to sit down and read all these in detail."

"I agree. I think those notebooks were important to him. They were arranged so neatly on his desk, like he had them there to consult in the planning of his work. In fact, they were the only thing on the desk apart from the laptop, and there was nothing in that I could see. But that kind of makes me want to ask the next question."

"Which is?"

"Well, if these are the notes for a book, which looks like a book about himself and his intimate thoughts…" she paused and looked up at him with her twinkling blue eyes and brushed a lock of hair from her face. "Where's the book?"

Sal stared at her.

"That… is a very good question," he said quietly.

Chapter 15

The Quiet Game

After spending an entire day at Terumoto's house and informing the chief inspector of what they had found in the notebooks, Sal had been given permission to take them and all the boxes of *shogi* magazines they had been investigating back to his home for analysis. The notebooks were too complicated for Penelope to read easily, so Sal was tasked with isolating and translating any points of interest, and they arranged to meet in a week to discuss the results.

The notebooks ran for several hundred pages, but how much was simply the author's stream-of-consciousness ramblings and how much actually meant anything and had been developed into any type of cohesive work was anybody's guess.

Sal had already more or less confirmed that the notes were definitely part of a plan for a book called *The Quiet Game,* and that it was most likely a distillation of the author's thoughts on life and *shogi* and their relationship. Several chapters seemed to develop the theme of prophylaxis, which an idea in chess for making seemingly 'quiet moves' that would disrupt the opponent's plans and making small, incremental improvements to one's position instead of looking for major moves. Terumoto seemed convinced that these 'hidden' moves were also the secret to a successful life. But they were only notes, and not a book. Yamashita had confirmed that according to the history on the laptop, which had not been wiped, there was no online copy of the book, and that if something like that did exist, it also was probably on paper, an idea that felt right to both Penelope and Sal.

In the meantime, Penelope had spent a lot of time thinking about the notebooks and what they had found, and looking at the photographs she had taken of the house. One bookcase, the largest one in the bedroom, had especially drawn her attention as, unlike all the others, that were crammed beyond capacity, this one had a strangely empty shelf and no dust on it, which indicated that it had either been cleaned or that whatever had been on it had been removed very recently.

There was something in this empty shelf and these photographs that she felt contained a key, a hint to the truth of the mystery and to why Terumoto and his son had been killed. If only she could figure out what that was...

A few days after the discovery of the notebooks, Penelope had come home to find Fei ensconced in her usual chair in the living room.

Today her friend had a more unusual piece of news, as well as a request.

"Suzume wants me to coach her," she said as she accepted the mug of coffee that Penelope had just made.

"Really? How do you feel about that?" she asked.

Fei was a senior and well-known player in the *shogi* world, and had held one of the top ranks among women players, the third *dan*, for many years. However, even she had to admit that her glory days as a player were behind her now. She rarely played tournaments anymore, yet she had also never accepted a coaching position, even though several schools had approached her to do so in the past.

"I said yes," she said happily. "I think she needs to get back to playing and concentrate on winning the next few tournaments so she can turn professional, if that's what she wants to do. So I said I would help her until she can find a better coach."

Penelope sighed. "Well, I guess you can use the spare bedroom. How about that? And this room, of course. You can't train her at your place, your aunt will be interrupting her with food every five minutes."

Fei grinned. "Thanks, that was my next question, if we could use your house. You don't mind having her around every day? It's going to be a bit intensive, I'm afraid. And it's easier for me than going to her place or finding a space somewhere."

Penelope waved the idea away. "No, of course not. I think you're right, it's exactly what she needs. She can come here. I will look after the food, and you two can just concentrate on your work. Don't worry about it."

Alphonse, her large black tomcat, came and rubbed himself on her legs, and Penelope bent down and scratched him behind his ears.

"Besides, she likes cats. That's lucky for you, isn't it?" she said, addressing the cat, who mewed appreciatively.

"OK," said Fei. "It's a deal. I'm not sure how much I can help her. I may need to get some help. But I want to try if that's what she wants. OK! Thank you. Let's see if we can't get this girl ready to win a few games then...."

Fei and Suzume wasted no time getting started. At 9 a.m. the next morning, they arrived in Penelope's living room carrying a huge pile of books and papers in shopping bags and proceeded to unpack everything on Penelope's dining table.

"This is so nice of you Penny-*sensei*. I don't know how to thank you," Suzume said with a smile.

Penelope gave her some coffee. "Thank Fei, she's doing all the hard work. You are welcome to come for as long as you need to. I'm happy to help, but that may just be in the kitchen. I don't know a *shogi* board from a cutting board."

Fei and Suzume moved all their books and a couple of *shogi* boards and laptops into the spare bedroom as Penelope had suggested, but they tended to spend most of their time playing and discussing games in the sunny living room, where Suzume could also be with her feline friends, who had taken an immense liking to the pretty young woman.

"So what's the plan then?" Penelope asked them as she stared at the mountain of *shogi* books on her table.

Fei grimaced and opened her laptop.

"The plan... if there is a plan... is to go through all the games Suzume has played over the last year to see what weaknesses she has. That's the first thing, it's called the Botvinnik Method, an idea I picked up from Western chess. I especially want to go over any games she lost and see what happened." She turned to Suzume, who was busy sorting the books into piles. "Then we are also going to analyze your main choice of openings and how you play them. And,

176

of course, we are going to look at several new ideas in professional games from the last few years, and solve a bucketload of puzzles every day, and other stuff. So don't worry… you won't be bored."

Suzume nodded happily, as she was familiar with various teacher training methods and trusted Fei's wisdom when it came to guiding her.

"Also, good news for you, I had a chat with Noguchi *sensei* yesterday, he said he is going to drop in and give you some training as well," added Fei.

Penelope had also met Noguchi-*sensei* in the past, a pleasant, slightly abstracted man in his early fifties who was completely obsessed with *shogi* and had been a professional player since he was a teenager. He was also a well-known coach who had helped many leading players in the past, so this was indeed good news for Suzume.

And so, over the next few days, the training camp got underway.

Suzume was scheduled to play two important tournaments in the next few months, and if she could win both, she had a good chance of being accepted into the professional ranks, according to Fei, who had been talking with the higher-up people in the *shogi* world to confirm what she needed to do. The first of these tournaments was in a month, so they had a lot of work to do to prepare for it.

Suzume seemed completely unfazed though, and not nervous at all about the daunting task in front of her. She would happily chat about other things and play with the cats in her free time, and neither Fei nor Penelope could detect any lingering negative effects caused by the recent death of her old trainer and boyfriend.

She would usually arrive at 9 a.m. every morning, stay till late at night, and occasionally sleep in the spare bedroom rather than return home. Mari would also drop in periodically to see how things were going, but she never stayed long as she was preparing for a major exhibition of her work which was going to be held in Osaka, so she was going to be out of town quite a bit over the next few weeks. She did promise to turn up for the tournament though, no matter what. She also thanked Penelope and Fei and agreed that this work was precisely what her niece needed.

For Penelope though, it was a minor and unexpected little incident towards the middle of the second week of their training camp that was to have a profound effect on her thinking about the Ripper case.

That day Fei and her protégé were sitting at the living room table as usual, working on a *shogi* puzzle. Two of Penelope's cats, Biscuit and Coco, were asleep, one on the edge of the table and another on one of the empty chairs. Suzume was staring at a position that Fei had set up on the board, and the latter was timing how long it would take her to solve it.

Penelope shooed Coco off her chair and sat down to join them for a moment before she started preparing the lunch.

"Do you recognize this?" asked Fei, nodding at the board.

"Me?" said Penelope. "How would I know it?"

"Well, you should, it's the 'Climbing Silver' opening. You know… CS…"

"Oh, is it?" asked Penelope, glancing at Suzume, who didn't look up from the board.

"You know, I have been meaning to ask you about that," said Penelope. "Why is it called that?"

"Climbing Silver?"

"Yes. It seems an odd name," she said.

Suzume looked up and pointed to the piece called the silver general on the board in front of her.

"Because this piece 'climbs' up the board, where it causes a lot of trouble. It's a good strategy. I often use it," she said.

"Oh, OK. I get it," said Penelope, nodding.

Suzume reached forward and moved a piece, and Fei stopped the timer she was using on her smartphone.

"Wrong?" asked Suzume with a frown.

"I'm afraid so," said Fei. "You should leave the gold general where it is, protecting the king. That's its job," said Fei.

"OK..." said Suzume.

Penelope went to the kitchen to make some omelets and salad for lunch. "This is all over my head, dears. I'll leave it to you," she said.

A few moments later, as she was just about to cut into a tomato, her hand froze as it held the knife. It was one of those moments she sometimes had when something that had long been in the back of her mind suddenly became clear.

She went back into the living room.

"So the role of the gold general piece in this opening is to protect the king?" she asked.

Fei and Suzume looked up at her startled.

"Yes, why?" asked Fei.

"So... it's a protective piece? That's why it doesn't move, right?"

"Right."

"So, it's a very *quiet* piece. Wouldn't you agree?" asked Penelope.

Fei nodded and laughed. "Sure. Very quiet. In this opening, its role is to protect the King. Is that important?" she said with a confused look.

Penelope stared at them and said nothing for a long moment, wiping her hands on a tea towel.

"Yes. Maybe…. Because… I just had an idea… Wow… Yes. I have to speak to Sal. I think. I'll go call him. Thank you!" she said happily, and left the room.

Fei and Suzume stared at each other and burst out laughing.

=====================

The two sisters sat in Mari's kitchen at the large white marble counter as the twilight gathered outside the big glass doors opening onto the garden. Outside, the first stars were just becoming visible above the hills of ancient Kamakura, and you could feel the old ghosts stirring in the shadows.

The taxi taking Junko to the airport had been called and her bags were packed and waiting at the door.

"When do you think you can come to Kamakura again?" asked Mari.

"I don't really know. It's hard to get away from auntie and uncle. They're getting on you know…."

Mari nodded. "Do you need any money?"

Junko laughed and looked a little offended. It was a sad laugh the way someone laughs at an ironic story.

"Money... it doesn't buy everything, you know," she said.

"I know... but if you need anything... you know I always..."

Junko cut her off.

"How about you buy me the last twenty years? How much does that cost? And maybe the next ten... which I will spend looking after these old people. Have you got that much?" Junko said, giving her sister an odd look.

Mari looked at the floor.

"I didn't know you felt like that. I thought you wanted this. You know. A family..."

Junko swirled the wine in her glass.

"Family is everything. We just have to do our best..." said Mari.

Junko nodded and her momentary anger faded away like a cloud drifting over a hill.

"I just miss her, you know. At least when I had her with me, it was easier, you know, dealing with these things."

These parting conversations with her sister had always been difficult, ever since they had been small and occasionally spent time apart.

They had grown up on an old farm, the only daughters of a father who had wanted sons and a mother who had always been disappointed she couldn't provide them. Together they had walked hand in hand along the icy roads to school every morning, and Junko, being several years older than her had always looked out for her and made sure she didn't fall into any of the roadside ditches and hadn't forgotten her lunch and a hundred other little things that young children did.

After school, there had been chores, and Junko had always done half of hers as well as her own, and eventually had made sure Mari had been looked after when their parents had died and they had gone to live with their aunt and uncle in Akita city, the prefectural capital.

Mari reached over and held her hand, conscious of the great debt that she owed her sister. Junko had always been her protector, the one who had made everything right, whereas she had, until recently, been the struggling artist, seen by many as just a stupid dilettante throwing away her life on daubs and drawings.

But Junko had never seen it like that.

In many ways, though, after their parents had passed away within a year of each other, they had felt a sense of freedom, not only from their expectations but even more from their disappointment. The farm had been sold, and the money had been used for their education and a little bit left over, which Mari had eventually given to Junko so that she could look after their aunt and uncle and Suzume without having to go out and work. She had also sent her much larger sums after her art had become successful, eventually enough to rebuild their relative's old house into two spacious, modern apartments where they could all live together but still have some privacy from each other, which was a common practice in Japan for people looking after aging relatives.

"Maybe we need to hire someone to help you," she said softly.

"Yes. I think it's getting to that stage now," said Junko reluctantly. "I don't know how long I can manage by myself some days…."

Mari knew that when she could come to Kamakura and see Suzume that these short breaks provided her with a welcome respite from her duties at home.

"OK. Let me make some inquiries then."

"Thanks. That would be good. There is just one other thing… I don't know. I've been thinking…."

"What about?" asked Mari.

Junko sighed. "We need to tell her, you know. Before she finds out on her own. She's getting older… and I'm worried."

Mari looked carefully at her sister and took a sip of her wine.

"I know."

There was resignation in her voice, and also a cold fear in her eyes.

"What do you think she will do when she finds out?" asked Junko.

Mari shook her head.

"I have no idea. But I think with everything that's happened recently… we should do it later. Not now. She's still getting over that man's death. He meant a lot to her… more than I thought, actually."

"That's true, I suppose," said Junko. "Anyway… I have to go. Let's talk about it later. Next time I come down. We can decide when's the right moment."

"OK. Let's do that. Are you sure you don't want me to drive you to the station?"

"No, it's OK. The taxi should be here any second."

Mari nodded, and standing up, she embraced her sister and walked with her to the door.

"I'm sorry," said Junko, brushing away a tear. "I didn't mean to… you know…"

"It's OK," said Mari, squeezing her hand. "I understand."

After her sister left, Mari went back into her studio, switched on the large fluorescent lights hanging overhead, and pushed another button on the remote control by the door, which caused the electric blinds to descend across the high windows and block out the night outside.

In the middle of the room was a large canvas she had been working on, and she now stood and stared silently at the work for several minutes before picking up a brush and squeezing some paint onto a small pallet by her side. This painting was something she was racing to get ready for the exhibition starting in Osaka in the next few weeks, and she had been working almost non-stop on it for days now and until late in the night.

The painting showed a man sitting by a river writing in a book and leaning against a large willow tree. His face was turned away towards the river, so just the side and back of his head were visible. Pages from the book lay scattered on the ground next to him, and a full moon shone bright and clear in the topmost branches. A moonlit path ran next to the tree and along the river into the distance, and the discarded pages of the book were being blown in the wind as far as the eye could see, rising into the night sky as if they were birds in flight.

Chapter 16

The Gold General

Contrary to the popular image held by most foreigners that the best season to visit Japan is during the cherry blossom time in spring, many Japanese prefer autumn. The weather during this season is milder, the days beautifully clear, and the autumn colors, the dazzling maples and golden yellow ginkgo trees that fill the ancient temples, particularly in places like the old capital of Kyoto, last much longer than the short few weeks of the cherry blossom season.

The first of Suzume's two important tournaments fell on just such a perfect, clear autumn day, the air crisp and cool, and the first of the maples beginning to turn red in the corner of Penelope's garden.

The tournament was being held in a large hall near Ochanomizu station in central Tokyo, an area Penelope knew well and liked. It was just up the road from Jimbocho, famous for its large number of second-hand book shops, and featured the ancient Kanda-Myojin shrine, dozens of shops selling musical instruments, and no less than three major universities around the old station, which for some reason always seemed to be undergoing some perpetual kind of major overhaul which had lasted at least the entire thirty years that Penelope had been resident in the country.

Suzume had stayed the night at Fei's house, where she had been forbidden to even look at a *shogi* board during the evening and had instead spent the time being overfed by Fei's Auntie Chen, who had, as always, served up enough food for ten people.

Sal had also volunteered to come up to Tokyo with them, so they all met at 6.30 a.m. at Kamakura station for the short trip to the capital on the express train, and then went straight to a cafe near the venue for a late breakfast.

Sal was in excellent spirits for someone self-described as 'not a morning person' and, if anything, was more excited than Suzume to attend the tournament.

"Maybe I should get out more," he smiled over his boiled egg and toast. "I'm seriously thinking of taking up this game more seriously."

Fei gave him an ironic look. "Well, it's maybe a bit less stressful than writing books about crime. Though I hear that pays better…."

"Yes, you could be right there. Anyway, when Suzume hear turns pro and sets the *shogi* world alight, I can get first dibs on her biography. What do you think, Suzume-san? Can I write your life history?"

Suzume blushed. "That would be a very short book," she said.

"Oh… leave that to me. I'm good at filling pages…" he smiled.

After breakfast and quite a lot of coffee, they made their way to the tournament venue around the corner, a large room in a modern complex that included a concert hall and

186

a theater. The room was already set up with over forty tables, and the officials were busy gathering around the arbiter's area and sorting out the players into their different groups. There were to be four groups playing today, and Suzume was in the most elite A group, which would be playing towards the front of the hall, with the finalists of the four divisions playing on the stage at the end of the day.

"Oh God," said Fei looking around. "This takes me back to my playing days when I was her age. I was so scared I couldn't sleep for a week before these things."

Penelope smiled. "You still won, though, I hear."

"Well, not all the time. Suzume has much better nerves than me. Just look at her…."

Penelope and Sal looked over at Suzume, who was calmly perusing the bookstall that had been set up in the lobby.

"She's looking forward to playing. That's all she wants to do," said Sal.

Fei nodded. "She has that way some people have of just thinking about the position. It's a gift. Once she gets in front of a board, she is totally unaware of her opponent and who they are. I wouldn't be surprised if she forgets what they even look like after the game. It's amazing to have that level of absorption."

"Sounds a bit spooky to me," said Sal.

"Me too," said Penelope, watching the players and their supporters filing into the hall.

Play began at 10 a.m. on the dot, and Suzume and the other players were sitting at their tables, ready and waiting when the chief arbiter climbed onto the stage and told them to start their clocks.

"Here we go…" whispered Sal, and the three of them began their tense wait at the back of the hall.

About five minutes later, Penelope saw Mari standing at the entrance and went over to greet her. She had just arrived on the bullet train from Osaka, a journey of about two hours, where she had been busy setting up her new exhibition, scheduled to start the following day.

"Sorry I'm late," she said, "I should have got the earlier train, but it was full. How is she doing?"

Penelope pointed towards Suzume at the front of the hall. Her arms were folded across her chest, and there was a completely unreadable expression on her face. Occasionally, she would sit up straighter, close her eyes, and remain like that until her opponent moved. Then her eyes would flutter open, and a quiet look, almost of happiness, would pass across her face, like the pieces were speaking to her and they had just done something wonderful.

"She looks so calm," said Mari with a wistful look.

Penelope nodded. "Not just calm… peaceful almost."

Each of the players had been given thirty minutes for their match, and there followed a thirty-second increment after that time expired, meaning that they would only have thirty seconds to make their next move or they would lose on time.

After about forty minutes or so, the very tense-faced young girl who had been playing Suzume stood up, bowed, and hurriedly made her way out of the hall. Suzume calmly finished packing away the pieces in their little plastic box, arranged it neatly in the center of the board, and then made her way to the arbiter's table to inform the waiting officials that she had won her first game.

"Congratulations," said Fei as she came over to greet them. "How did it go?"

Suzume shrugged and smiled. She was wearing a long dark skirt, a light blue blouse with butterflies embroidered on it, and a little gold bracelet with a maple leaf design that her mother had given her for luck when she had last visited.

"She made a mistake in the opening, and then it kind of went downhill for her after that. I don't think she was fully aware of the variation... anyway, it didn't take all that long. I'm going to buy some tea."

And with that, she walked into the lobby and headed for the vending machines.

"Looks like you've done a good job, Fei-san," said Mari. "Thank you so much for coaching her."

"Oh, don't mention it," said Fei. "Most of the time, she just teaches herself."

Mari smiled. "Yeah... she's always been a bit like that. And she seems to remember everything... at least about *shogi*. She has no idea about her schedule or homework or what she did yesterday, but she can remember every move of a game she played five years before. It's weird...."

"I know a few people like that, actually," said Fei, looking at Penelope and Sal, who were just leaving the playing hall and deep in conversation about something.

Suzume returned with her tea, and a few minutes later, the arbiters posted the matches for the second round. Fei and Suzume walked over to where the crowd had gathered around the announcement, and Suzume took one short glance and left for her designated table at the front of the hall without a word.

Fei came back frowning to where Mari was standing.

189

"Well. This one is going to be a lot tougher. She's got Tomoko Deguchi, who only needs one more tournament win to turn professional herself. She is going to need a bit of luck here…."

Mari nodded. "Where are Penelope and Sal?"

Fei shrugged. "They went outside. I guess they'll be back soon enough."

Outside in the bright autumn sunshine, Sal and Penelope were standing on the steps of the hall with some cans of coffee they had just bought from the vending machine.

"So," Sal was remonstrating, "you are saying, if I've got this right, that there are two killers, and that one is protecting the other. Is that right?" asked Sal with a confused expression.

"Basically… yes."

"So tell me again then… *how* do you arrive at this conclusion?"

Penelope opened her can of coffee, which was still too hot to drink, and placed it on the banister next to her.

"I think the killer, the second killer anyway, is telling us. I think the message is hidden in the *shogi* piece he leaves with the victims."

"The gold general?"

"Yes," said Penelope. "The gold general. I don't think enough attention has been given to this piece and its meaning."

"What are you saying, though? I know it's an important piece in *shogi*. I mean, it's not a piece you want to lose and then see it deployed against you…."

"That's true… but I don't think that's all there is to it. I'll tell you what I think," said Penelope. "I thought when I first

190

heard about this piece being left with the victims, that it was just a convenient, somewhat creepy way for the killer to identify themselves. Like it was a calling card. Rather cool, right?"

"Sure, it is. That's what I always thought too. That's why I always thought the killer was a *shogi* player, and Terumoto always identified himself as such, of course. And by the way, I'm still convinced he killed his wife," said Sal.

Penelope nodded. "Actually… I agree with you. He may well have killed his wife. Probably to run off with his mistress. He may also have had an accomplice. Who was the woman who called the *shogi* club that night? Or maybe it was him, pretending to be a woman caller. The only problem was that he was a lot worse at concocting an alibi than he was at playing *shogi*. That was a really hamfisted affair. But there was something else about that killing that caught my eye too. Have you seen this?"

She reached into her rucksack and handed Sal a large yellow manilla envelope.

Sal put down his coffee, and extracted a set of black and white photographs from it.

"I got these from Yamashita-san yesterday. He wasn't real keen to hand them over until I told him they were for your research."

Sal went through the photographs carefully.

"Ah… The first crime scene, Terumoto's wife, Akiko. Yeah, I've seen these before. When I was writing my book."

Penelope smiled, "OK, I won't ask you how. They're supposed to be a big police secret. At the time, no one knew about the *shogi* piece left with each of the victims."

Sal grinned. "Yeah, I know a lot of big police secrets. They are not so hard to find out if you know the right cop. Anyway, what's your point?"

Penny pointed to the top photograph.

"These are all pictures that show the *shogi* piece and the scene of the murder. Where is the gold general?"

"The gold general?" Sal looked at the photo and pointed. "Here. On the victim's back."

"Right. Because she is lying face down on the floor, and the piece was placed on her back."

"OK, what are you getting at?"

She showed him the second photograph.

"What are these?" she said, pointing.

Sal looked confused. "A bunch of other *shogi* pieces lying on the floor next to her body."

Penelope nodded and showed him the third photograph.

"And what about this?"

Sal stared. "It looks like the side of a *shogi* board, on the table above the body."

Penelope nodded. "That's the only photograph that shows the *shogi* board at all. The police took photos of the body, and the pieces on the floor, and the gold general on her back. That's all, though."

"OK, so what?"

"So, what if the gold general fell from the board onto the body accidentally?"

"Unlikely. The gold general was used in all the killings."

"But only the first killing was done by Terumoto, right? And as far as we know, he was only planning to kill his wife, no one else, right?"

Sal nodded. "Right. As far as we know."

192

"So," said Penelope, raising her eyebrow and pointing to the gold general in the first photo. "Why leave a calling card, then? If you are not going to kill again? There's no need, is there?"

Sal stared at the photograph and then at Penelope.

"I never thought of that," he smiled.

Penelope tapped on the photograph again with her finger.

"Neither did the police. One more thing too."

"What?"

"The gold general was found lying on the back of the victim, where it might have landed had it fallen from the table, perhaps during a scuffle with the killer or afterward. Here's a question. Where were the other gold generals on the other victims found?"

Sal's eyes opened wide.

"In their hands…" he whispered. "Where they were… placed."

Penelope looked at him and smiled.

"Exactly. The first one fell there by accident. The others were deliberately placed in the victim's hands. And if they were placed there… *now* they have a meaning. What this tells us is that there is *another* killer who has this information, who knows what piece was on the original body, and who wants to connect all the killings together. So what I am saying is that it is highly likely that the second killer was there, at Akiko's death, where they either watched it happen, helped it happen or did it themselves. They were there."

Sal stared at her, alarmed.

"Or they had access to these photographs or the crime scene and saw the body for themselves. Are you talking about a cop?"

Penelope nodded. "Maybe a cop... or someone else who was there... with Terumoto. Someone who would have seen it, and then used the information later when they killed again. Remember, there was no letter with the first victim. That only started with the second. So it makes sense to say that Akiko's death was a standalone killing, not done by someone planning a series. The second killer then used their knowledge of the *shogi* piece on Akiko's body to help get Terumoto off the hook."

"To protect him... is that what you are saying?"

Penelope gave him an encouraging look, like he was a particularly slow student who was just beginning to catch up.

"Here is another thing to think about too. Let's forget about the gold general for a moment. And forget about it being the killer's calling card. That's established by the letters anyway, so we don't even need the gold general on the body at all, do we? It's superfluous."

Sal nodded. "That's true. We don't need it. Are you saying it's a red herring? Something to lead the police in the wrong direction?"

Penelope shook her head and tapped her finger on the photograph.

"No, Sal. Not at all. I'm telling you the *opposite*. It's the killer's *name*...."

Sal's mouth dropped open. "Their *name*?"

"Yes. CS. 'Climbing Silver'. Right? Think about it. What's the gold general's role in the 'Climbing Silver' opening? What does it *do*?"

Penelope folded her arms and waited while Sal thought about it.

194

"It doesn't do anything, straight away at least. It stays on the back rank," he said after a while.

"Exactly. Where is it, though?"

Sal paused. "Next to the king, I think. Yes… Oh shit. Yes. It protects the king."

Penelope tapped him on the arm.

"And who is the king in this killer's life?" she asked.

Sal smiled. "Terumoto… it's Terumoto."

"You have it, I think. That's who the killer is. They are Terumoto's protector. And they were there with him when he killed his wife. Maybe they even helped."

"Wow, Penny…" Sal said admiringly.

"And that's why I am saying this case is all about protection. The killer is protecting Terumoto, at least in the first three killings after the wife dies. But in the second three, the gold general motif continues. Toyozaki dies because he is on the case and a very good detective. He might have been able to figure things out about the ensuing killings given the chance. Then Terumoto's son dies, and then the father. The killer is no longer protecting Terumoto, obviously. They are protecting *someone else*…."

"And Terumoto the son, and the father… they are a threat to that person… is that it?"

Penelope smiled.

"You were always my favorite student, Sal. Did you know that?

Chapter 17.

The Dead Speak

Penelope and Sal rejoined the others in the playing hall just as the second round of games was concluding. All of the other players had left their tables, but there was still one game going, and this was between Suzume and her opponent. An arc of other players stood around them at a discreet distance, quietly watching these two advanced players as they made their final moves. The atmosphere in the playing hall was palpably taut.

"They're both playing on the thirty-second increment," said an obviously nervous Fei. "It's not going to go on much longer."

"I think I'm going to die of nerves," said Mari, who had a small towel in her hands which she was squeezing compulsively every few seconds.

Penelope and Sal looked over to where they sat and felt the tension mounting with each move and also the deep silence, where apart from the soft 'click' of the pieces being placed on their squares, you could now hear a pin drop.

With both players only having thirty seconds to move or lose the game, the chances of one or both of them making a fatal error had grown exponentially. These sorts of games, tight contests that go down to the wire, often depended not so much on who was the better player, but on which of them had the better nerves.

Suzume's opponent was older and more experienced, but she was hunched over the board in a manner that betrayed real panic, and was slapping down her pieces with some ferocity whenever she moved.

On the other hand, Suzume was sitting back in her chair with an air of complete calm, her arms folded across her chest and only reaching for her piece with a mere second to spare before sitting back again and resuming her pose. The seconds ticked by, and each time, just before their time expired, the players managed another move, and the cycle would continue.

And then, almost unexpectedly, it was over.

A few of the arbiters were also standing a short distance away watching the player's clocks when one stepped forward and said something to them. The two women immediately cleared the board of its pieces and packed them into the little plastic box, which they left neatly in the center of the board for the next match.

Suzume's opponent stood and bowed, and walked calmly out of the playing hall without a backward glance.

"She lost on time. It was a pity," said Suzume with a shy smile as she joined them.

Fei's hand flew to her mouth, and her aunt reached out and hugged her.

"My God, Suzume. Well done!" said Fei, who was ecstatic.

A small group of other players gathered around them to congratulate Suzume on her win, and she smiled and went off to talk to them.

"Those are people from her old school, I think," said Mari turning to Fei. "Well… what do you think, Fei-san? Has she got a chance?"

Fei nodded and smiled.

"If she can beat Tomoko Deguchi, I would say she can beat anyone here. Yes, I think she has a good chance, actually."

"She looked pretty impressive to me," said Sal. "I don't know how she can handle pressure like that. It looks like she is in the zone or something. Is she always like that?"

"Yeah. Pretty much. Especially in front of a *shogi* board. I always think she looks like someone has hypnotized her…" said Mari with a laugh.

The lunch break followed, and the players assembled in the hall again.

This time Suzume shocked everybody by destroying another older player in less than thirty moves, and was back with them again within half an hour, one of the first players to finish their games.

She now had three clear wins and one game to go, and was tied for the lead with two other players, all of whom were much older and more experienced than she was. That being said, there was a buzz of conversation going around the playing hall about her, and several people in the upper echelons of the Tokyo *shogi* world had sought Fei out to ask about her.

When the final game began, the four of them stood at the rear of the hall as before, waiting for the outcome with nothing short of dread. It seemed unbelievable that Suzume, with all the odds stacked against her and the trauma of recently losing her teacher in such a hideous way, should be able to perform at this level against seasoned veterans in the top division, a group that she had only very recently been able to join after her late teacher had interceded with the game's hierarchy to recommend her. This time, however, Fei thought Suzume's luck might have run out.

She had drawn Inaba Mitsuko as her opponent, a player some ten years older than her and one of the strongest amateur women players in the Kanto region, which included the whole of the four prefectures surrounding Tokyo.

"Is she any good?" asked Penelope naively.

"Good?" said Fei with a frown. "Normally, I would say she should eat Suzume for breakfast. I say 'should' because you never know. But I've played her once myself, and she wiped me out on that occasion, about two years ago. We will just have to wait and see though."

Time for the nervous spectators passed slowly, but for the players, it seemed like only a few minutes had elapsed. One by one they finished their games, and the hall gradually cleared around Suzume and her opponent again. The clock had gradually ticked down to its final seconds and once again both players finished their allotted thirty minutes and began to play on the dreaded thirty-second increment.

This time there was no sign of visible panic at all though. The two women seemed to be floating in a bubble of complete calm, quietly clicking their pieces onto their squares with slow, unhurried movements, usually with just a second or even less to spare. After ten minutes on increment, all of the other players had now finished and were standing with the arbiters in a wide arc around Suzume and Inaba Mitsuko, who played on, completely oblivious of them.

Ten more minutes passed like this and the crowd was absolutely silent, awed by the intricate tactical battle the two players were engaged in. Fei and Mari had managed to get to the front of the crowd where they could see the players clearly, and others were even standing on chairs behind the other spectators to get a view of the game.

On and on, each time just within the allotted time, the players made their moves, with Suzume sitting once again with her arms folded and an expression of complete tranquillity on her face, her right hand rising gracefully to pick up her piece and place it gently on the board without the slightest sign of rushing.

And then, with just a few seconds to spare on her clock, they saw Inaba raise her piece in the air… and then, ever so slightly… she hesitated.

She then played her move, and the crowd waited for Suzume's response, which came just a few seconds later.

Inaba stared at Suzume's piece and seemed frozen in her seat.

She looked up at Suzume, and then back down at the board. With but a single second left on her clock, instead of moving, she bowed her head and in a clear voice said:

"*Makemashita. Omodeto gozaimasu.*" I have lost. Congratulations.

The crowd started to clap quietly and Mari hugged Fei, who looked like she was about to burst into tears.

Suzume was pronounced the winner both of the game and of her division.

She was on her way.

=====================

Chief Inspector Yamashita was a patient and thorough officer, trained in the management of men and large police operations, and respected by his high-ranking bosses as one of the safest pairs of hands in running a murder investigation that existed in the service.

But he had other accomplishments as well.

He was also a gifted cellist and writer, and had penned a number of successful mystery novels in his spare time, as well as being one of the only members of the force ever to have graduated from the profiling school run by the FBI at their Quantico headquarters in the United States.

When he was in charge of an investigation, especially one as long-running and complicated as the Ripper case, he obeyed the one golden rule his old mentor Toyozaki had repeatedly told him: don't rush.

"If you rush, you will miss something, and if you miss something in cases like this, it can have you chasing your tail for years until you discover your mistake." This was the maxim his old boss had drilled into his protégé's head.

Nevertheless, at this moment, he was at his wit's end as to what to do.

The killer had indicated clearly in his last letter that they were going to kill someone else, and so far this murderer had been a man of his word.

He had sat with that final letter for two weeks now, going over and over it for some clue as to what it meant, and had shown it to every expert in the force, even having it translated for some of his old friends in the FBI to cast an eye over.

Nothing had been of any use.

The randomness, the remorseless precision and the lack of clues in any shape or form provided by the Ripper had left both himself and the rest of the police force completely stymied for any kind of useful response. There was simply nothing to go on, and so that night he had concluded that there was nothing for them to do but to wait for the next victim to turn up and hope that for once, just once, the killer made some mistake.

He left the office that night at the unprecedented hour of 5 p.m., much to the delight of some of his underlings who felt that they could not go home until the boss did. He caught a passing bus the short distance to his home near the beautiful Meigetsu-in temple, beloved by all in the misty rainy season each June for its beautiful hydrangeas and where he had lived in solitude for so many years with only his cat Watson and the temple bell for company.

He stopped by a nearby supermarket and bought an altogether too-expensive bottle of a Californian cabernet he liked, and a steak to go with it. Then he headed home to cook and to forget about work for the first time in weeks.

He had, to put it mildly, had enough.

At home, the confirmed bachelor, who relished the chance to be alone with his many hobbies and interests, put an old LP of Bach's orchestral works on his turntable, opened the wine, and cooked his steak with rosemary to the accompaniment of the beautiful violin concerto A minor.

Dinner finished, he sat down on his comfortable leather couch and watched the international news on the BBC, and wondered if he could find something interesting on Netflix. He was too tired to do anything else that night, and all he wanted to do was to drink too much and watch something mindlessly entertaining. Everything else could wait.

About two hours later he woke up suddenly to find that he had dozed off completely and that his mobile phone was vibrating on the coffee table in front of him.

He checked the name displayed on the phone and cursed silently.

"Yamashita," he said curtly.

"Sir, it's Yokota," came the apologetic voice of his young detective sergeant. "Very sorry to disturb you sir, but it looks like we have another body. Another Ripper case, I'm afraid…."

Yamashita slumped back in his seat.

"You might be interested to hear this, sir. There has been a bit of a twist with this one."

"Just tell me," said Yamashita, trying to clear his foggy, sleep-ridden head.

There was a slight pause as the younger officer tried to find the right words.

"The body, sir. It's the Ripper."

An hour later, showered and dressed in his suit again, Yamashita stood, coffee in hand in the darkened garden of an old apartment complex in the popular Shonan area, not far from the famous Hase temple.

In front of him, a large white tent was being erected by the forensic crew around the recently discovered body of a man in his late fifties, who had apparently jumped from the tenth floor of the apartment block to his death in a small children's playing area beneath.

Detective Sergeant Yokota, noticing his boss standing over the body in the tent, went over and passed him a small plastic evidence envelope that contained a document bearing the all too familiar brushwork of the Ripper on his usual stationery.

Under the bright fluorescent lights, Yamashita paused to read.

Dear little policemen,

I really have no words to tell you how disappointed I am in you.
Despite my generous offer in my previous letter, once again, you have let me down.
Couldn't you at least have made an effort? It wasn't asking too much of you to figure it out, after all. I would have come willingly had you done so.
I guess that was asking too much.
Anyway, in the end, I have saved you the trouble. The body you are looking at is indeed my own.
All the people who needed to die are now dead, including myself!
As I have always said, the police are incapable of protecting anybody.

Farewell, and I hope you learned something.

CS

Yamashita finished reading and passed the evidence bag back to Yokota.

"Where was this found?"

"On the kitchen table, in his apartment upstairs sir."

Yamashita stared at the body where it lay on the hard dark earth of the little playground, waiting for the forensic team to finish and the coroner to arrive, which he figured would be Dr. Taguchi in this case, as Fei only attended the day shift.

The man was dressed in a white business shirt, dark pants and was wearing a pair of cheap black business shoes. His short black hair was greying slightly at the temples, and his face looked thin and drawn.

"Do we know who this is?" he said, turning to Yokota.

Yokota reached into his pocket and pulled out his notebook.

"Yes sir. His wallet was in his pocket. Meet Taniyama Rintaro, fifty-eight years old, who lived up there on the tenth floor," he pointed up at an apartment close to the roof of the building with his pen. "We are trying to find next of kin, and interviewing the neighbors."

"Taniyama?"

"Yes sir."

Yamashita looked up at the balcony from where the man had fallen.

"Why do I know that name…" he said aloud.

Yokota shook his head. "Not sure, sir. We can run his details when we get back to the station if you like."

Yamashita shook himself as if from an unpleasant dream. "Let's have a look at his apartment."

The lift to the tenth floor was an old narrow contraption with only room for two people, and the dead man's apartment lay in the middle of the complex along a long open corridor.

The door was open and a uniformed officer was waiting for them with a couple of forensic techs who were dusting for fingerprints on the balcony.

The uniformed officer gave Yamashita a sharp salute.

"Thanks. You can wait outside," Yamashita said.

He began to look around the apartment, which was an old two-bedroom affair with a living room with a hardwood floor. The other two rooms were covered in inexpensive but clean tatami mats, like a lot of old apartments like this were.

"Did he own this place? Or was it rented?" Yamashita asked.

"He owned it sir, according to the building records. He's been here around thirteen years or so. Unmarried. Not sure about work, but we'll find out. I suggest you have a look in here," he said pointing at one of the rooms.

Yamashita nodded, and they went into what looked like the man's spare bedroom where there was a desk and chair and a wall of bookcases.

There was a *shogi* board on the desk with a single piece in the middle of it.

"The gold general, sir," said Yokota quietly.

Yamashita nodded.

"So I see."

Next to the board was a neat stack of thick art paper, with a brush laying neatly on top and a black inkstone with a bottle of cheap calligraphy ink.

Yokota bent down, picked up a small black rucksack lying next to the desk, and opened it.

"Sir..." he said, opening the top of the rucksack and holding it out for his boss to see.

Yamashita peered inside and saw a large builder's hammer.

"Bag it and give it to forensics," he said.

Yokota took the bag out into the next room and left him alone.

Yamashita sighed and went over to the bookcase and looked at the various *shogi* books, taking a few off the shelf and leafing through them. He opened the desk draws one by one, and pulled them out to inspect the bottoms.

Yokota poked his head around the door.

"Sir... something else that might be of interest," he said, nodding back into the living room.

Yamashita followed him.

"In the bathroom, sir, several bottles of these," he said, holding up a white plastic bottle of pills with an orange lid.

"Several receipts also sir, on the table, appear to be from the main hospital in Kamakura. This is Cytoxan..." he said, passing the pill bottle to Yamashita, who inspected the label.

"Do we know what these are for?"

"I saw these in my uncle's place, sir. He had prostate cancer. I think it's for chemotherapy."

Yamashita sat down on one of the dining room chairs and put his head in his hands.

"Final act, I would say, sir. Cancer is a nasty way to die," said Yokota.

"Maybe. It does rather look like that," said Yamashita noncommittally.

The apartment was neat and tidy, and the resident had clearly gone to some bother to keep it that way. The dishes were all washed in the sink, and the refrigerator and the pantry were well stocked with enough food for several days.

Yamashita looked into the bedroom and saw a set of futons folded neatly in the corner of the room, and in the middle of the floor was a small folding table with a laptop on it.

Yamashita sat down on the cushion in front of the table and opened it. There was no passcode.

Inside there was a mass of files, and when he looked at the browser history he found a long list of press articles about the Ripper case.

"OK. I want this thing back at the station please, and also pull this whole place apart, Yokota. I mean, everything. Let's see if there is anything useful here. Whatever you find, bag it and bring it to the station. I'm going to have another look at the body."

"You think it's him, sir? The Ripper?"

Yamashita paused and looked at him.

"Never rush, Yokota. Never rush…" he said with a slight smile and left the detective alone to get on with his work.

He returned downstairs in the claustrophobic elevator, and went outside to the tent where the coroner had just ordered the body to be placed on a folding gurney ready for transport to the police mortuary.

The coroner, Dr. Taguchi, an old friend, looked up and smiled.

"Well, good evening Eiji," he said. "You must be happy. This is the Ripper, I believe…."

Yamashita smiled.

"So people keep telling me. Can I have a look at him?"

"Be my guest," said Taguchi, unzipping the dark plastic body bag from head to foot so the chief inspector could see.

Yamashita stepped up to the gurney and got his first good look at the man they had been searching for in vain for the last eighteen years.

He was clean-shaven with a short, business-like haircut and slightly greying dark hair. His eyes were open and staring and the front of his shirt was covered with blood. Yamashita reasoned he had landed on his back, as the face and chest were relatively unmarked.

"Looks like any other salaryman, doesn't he? Just goes to show you can never tell who you are living next door to."

"That's the truth," said Yamashita grimly. "I gather he had some ID on him?"

"Yes." Taguchi pointed to a wallet that was lying on the white folding table in a plastic evidence bag.

Yamashita opened it up, took out the contents, and spread them on the table. He found a driver's license and held it up.

"Taniyama Rintaro…" he said out loud.

He also examined a health card and several points cards from local supermarkets and other shops.

Yamashita returned the wallet to the plastic evidence bag and looked carefully at the body. He opened the zip a little further and looked up at Taguchi.

"Shoes?" he said.

Taguchi nodded. "That's what I thought too."

"Did he wear glasses?"

"If these were his, he did. We found them a few meters away from the body."

He indicated another plastic bag on the table which had a pair of glasses with heavy black plastic frames.

"Can you see if these were for reading or for long distance?" he asked.

"I don't know, but you could ask your very efficient DS to find out, I reckon. Either way, it's a bit odd. That being said... it does happen."

Yamashita nodded. Although suicides were common in Japan, it was extremely unusual for someone to jump wearing either his shoes or his glasses. Nearly all people who jumped to their death, either in front of trains or from heights, took off their shoes and glasses first.

This behavior was so common it was one of the first things investigators at train stations looked for in order to establish whether the death had been an accident or not, and it was not at all uncommon in these cases to find a pair of shoes sitting neatly on the edge of the platform with their glasses, if they wore them, tucked inside.

Taniyama Rintaro had done neither of these things.

Yamashita pointed at the wallet in the bag.

"That's also weird. Why take your wallet?"

"Maybe he was in a hurry to get to the shop?" said Dr. Taguchi, with a dark smile.

Chapter 18

Dead Man's Shoes

Sal removed the cork from the bottle of champagne with a satisfying 'shush' and poured everyone a glass.

"I think someone's done that before," said Penelope.

"I won't deny I have some expertise on the champagne front," Sal smiled. "During the days when I was your impoverished student, professor, I moonlighted as a waiter at an expensive French place in Ginza. I opened crates of the stuff."

"So you are one of those wine snobs, are you?" asked Fei.

"Something like that. I know my bordeaux from my cabernet anyway… I just can't afford either of them these days."

"Somehow I think, tales of your present-day poverty are exaggerated. Didn't you just buy a second house in Nagano?"

Sal shook his head. "I need that so I can hunt for food… it's just a shack," he joked.

"A hunting lodge…" asked Penelope.

"Something like that…."

"What do you hunt in Nagano? Chinese tourists?" asked Fei.

Sal laughed. "I guess the hunting is better up north. My Dad told me he used to hunt for bear up in Akita and Morioka."

"Yes, I think a lot of folk are into hunting up there. Mari's sister said their father used to be a hunter. Lots of people with guns...." said Penelope.

"Yes, it's a nightmare for the police, too... but at least not as bad as in America." said the chief inspector.

Sal raised his glass.

"So, are we celebrating or not?" he asked.

"We should be," said Penelope. "Especially you. It's the end of a long road for you, and the police...." she said, looking at Yamashita, who looked like he had something on his mind. "But I get the feeling Eiji-san has something to tell us?"

"Eiji always has something up his sleeve," said Fei, who was sitting next to the chief inspector on the couch.

"That's only occasionally true." said the inspector, as he clinked glasses with Sal and Penelope. "I'm grateful you could all make it," he said quietly.

It was getting dark early this time of year, and they hadn't been able to see the maples in the inspector's garden, but it was still always pleasant to receive an invitation to his house, and to have a chance to talk over a meal. This time the inspector had prepared the food himself, albeit with most of it coming pre-cooked from a department store in town.

"So is everybody happy down in policeland?" asked Sal with a smile. "I mean, now you've wrapped it all up?"

Yamashita shrugged. "My bosses are happy. They usually are when they are not in the firing line from the media.

Everybody is glad to put the case to bed. I guess I should be too…."

Penelope, who, like Fei, knew him well, gave him a sideways look.

"Are you happy, though? Something tells me… you're not happy…."

"He's a policeman. They're never happy," quipped Sal, downing his champagne.

Yamashita put his glass on the coffee table and clasped his hands.

"Taniyama Rintaro," he said.

"AKA, the Ripper," interjected Sal, refilling his glass.

"What about him?" asked Penelope.

Yamashita frowned. "You know, we had him on our list right at the beginning of all this. It took me a while to twig to who he was. He was Akiko Terumoto's lover. I didn't remember who he was at first. That should be enough to disturb anyone. If we had woken up to him earlier a lot of people would still be alive."

"Maybe so, but nobody had him on the radar. I didn't either," said Sal. "And when you think about it, he had the perfect motive. Revenge."

Yamashita nodded.

"Well… you're right as it happens. Of course, he never killed Akiko. We know that because he had an alibi that night, which was…."

"Playing *shogi* in Tokyo till late. That's where he met Akiko. He used to be a coach at Terumoto's school. At least according to what I read in Sal's book," offered Penelope.

"True. He was infatuated with her. Never got married after she died. Rather sad in a way. We found some photographs of her next to where he slept."

"I can understand him killing Terumoto the father, and maybe the son, but what about the other murders? What was his motive for those?" asked Fei.

Yamashita smiled bitterly. "As Sal said, we never had him on our radar for those. I mean, why would he want to kill the Enamoto couple and Watanabe, the first three? What possible motive would he have? According to the reports, we did speak to him at the time, but the guy has been a virtual recluse since Akiko's death. He never went out, except to play *shogi* once a week. Just like Terumoto senior, actually. Sure, he had no alibi, so to speak, but neither does anyone else who stays at home in this city. So he was never pursued," he sighed.

"I think the Enamoto couple may have known something about his affair with Akiko which he didn't want known, after all, they were Akiko's neighbors. Killing them may have been to stop them from talking. Killing Watanabe after that was simply to continue the *shogi* motif and throw everyone off the scent, to point the police away from considering what the Enamotos really knew. Which he seems to have accomplished. After the first crime, information about Tanimoto and Akiko was leaked to the media, who lapped it up. It was thought at the time that the leak came from the police. Tanimoto's reputation was thoroughly trashed and he was fired from his job at the time. If young Enamoto leaked it, or Tanimoto thought he had, that would be a powerful motive."

"So what about the other murders then? The final three? Why come back and start again when you have gotten away with it?" asked Fei.

Yamashita shrugged. "Simple. Like Sal said. Revenge. He blamed Terumoto for his life taking the turn it had, hated him for being in the way between him and Akiko, and most of all for killing her. There are a dozen possible motives there. He wanted all of them dead. He killed the son to make Terumoto suffer like he had when he lost Akiko. And then he killed him as well, obviously out of revenge. And, of course, he did not want to be suspected by a good detective like Toyozaki, who might have joined the dots, so he made sure he got rid of him first. Toyozaki also interviewed him during the initial investigation into Akiko and gave him quite a rough time. He might have borne a grudge."

"But why wait eighteen years?" asked Penelope.

"Good question. But he had a good reason for wrapping things up, something that prompted him to seek retribution before it was too late…."

"Bowel cancer," said Fei. "Dr. Taguchi told me. He had about three months to live, according to the autopsy."

"He got rid of all the people he hated first. Very neat…" said Sal.

Yamashita looked up at him.

"Just the word I was thinking of… neat. Neat and tidy. No loose ends. The murder weapon and the writing equipment was all there, and his laptop was full of files about the killings. He was obviously keeping a track of things."

Penelope cocked her head to one side and smiled at him.

"You know, I know you hate neat. Especially *too* neat. And I hate neat as well," she said. "So, what's bothering you?"

The inspector reclined back onto the couch, and clasping his hands behind his head, stared up at the ceiling.

"Shoes," he said finally. "Shoes… and neat."

Sal laughed. "Shoes? Seriously?"

Yamashita nodded. "I've been doing this job a long time. A very long time. And this country, it has its little quirks. Most of Asia does. But one thing the Japanese do more than anyone else… is neat," he gave Sal a serious look. "And they take off their shoes before they die. Especially if they commit suicide. And they don't take their shoes off when they come home and then put them on again before they jump off their balcony. So yes, shoes. Shoes bother me."

"Not everyone takes their shoes off. Besides, going on to the balcony is technically *outside*. I have outside slippers to wear when I go out onto my balcony. Most people do. I don't go out there in socks. I think you are overthinking it, Eiji-san." said Sal.

"Well, a good ninety percent committing suicide *do* take their shoes off. It's always been a thing here. You know that," said Yamashita.

"And why do people do that?" said Fei. "I know I've seen it often enough on TV dramas. I've often wondered why… why take off your shoes?" said Fei.

"So as not to carry dirt from one world to the next. Samurai used to do the same thing before committing ritual suicide. You take off your shoes so you do not carry impurities with you into heaven," Penelope said. She leaned forward in her chair and gazed at Yamashita.

"And he didn't do that, did he?"

216

Yamashita nodded. "He did not."

"And that's why you're not happy," she said.

"That's why I'm not happy," he repeated with a smile.

"Well, I say forget about it. He's just one of the ten percent that didn't get the memo. He killed himself, he left you a note, he even left you his favorite murder weapon. That seems enough to me," said Sal.

"You're right. It should be. We should all eat, drink and be merry…after all, it's over finally. But there was a couple of other weird little things…."

"I'm going to regret asking this… what?" asked Sal.

"He had a little scratch of white paint from the balcony railing on the back of his belt."

"From when he climbed over it?"

"Why would it be on the back of his belt, then? Wouldn't it be on the front? And also a small circular mark on the front of his shirt and a bruise under it in the same place."

"And what do you think that was from?"

"No idea," said Yamashita. "I just don't like loose ends."

"Obviously not," said Fei. "But as they don't add up to anything, I think we should just be happy the guy is dead."

Yamashita nodded and looked at Penelope, who seemed lost in thought.

"Anyway, like you say," he said. "Let's forget about it."

They spent the rest of the evening talking about other things, deliberately avoiding the subject of the Ripper and his murderous reign, and they all left that night feeling better for the evening.

As they were leaving, Fei noticed Penelope having a word with Yamashita about something in the kitchen and went over to them on the pretext of saying goodbye.

"Family records?" Yamashita was saying. "Yeah, of course. We can get those. Do you want me to email you a copy of them?"

"Yes, please," said Penelope.

"And what are you guys talking about?" said Fei.

"Oh, nothing. Just something I wanted to know," replied Penelope vaguely.

"Don't tell me you two are still working on this case?" she frowned, as Yamashita and Penelope looked guiltily at each other.

"She wanted to know if you were related to any particularly nasty Chinese emperor. Like Empress Wu. I'm going to check it out. I want to know too…" quipped Yamashita.

"Hmmm… I think I am related to Ghenghis Khan, actually. But so is half of China, it would appear." she smiled. "Thank you for dinner anyway."

"Don't mention it," said Yamashita with a mock bow.

Sal walked Penelope and Fei out to where they were waiting for their taxi to appear.

"You know, I really rather liked your theory," he said.

"Which one was that? I think I had about five…" smiled Penelope.

"You know what I mean. The story about protection, and the reason that the killer started again after so long. I thought that made a lot of sense."

"Well… thank you, Sal. That's nice of you. Except I seem to have got it wrong."

"Maybe… Don't mention it."

"But you know…" she said. "There is one thing I would like to know."

"What's that?"

Penelope paused.

"I'd like to know who that girl was. The one in the picture in Terumoto's study, playing *shogi* with him. They just looked so happy together. You know, I think that there was another picture too. The one that used to hang in the living room."

"I thought that was the one he put in his study?"

She shook her head.

"Nope. The frame size was different to the mark on the wall in the living room. The one in the living room is the one I want to see. I'm just wondering though, if they were the same. One for upstairs, and one for downstairs. I think she was special. There were other photos of her too…."

"Well, he was supposed to be a bit of a ladies' man back in the day."

"Still, I get the feeling this one was different somehow."

"I would say so. I don't have any pictures of my ex-girlfriends on the wall at home," said Sal.

The taxi pulled up in front of them and the driver popped open the back door.

"You know, you probably just don't have enough wall for all of them…" said Fei with a laugh.

Sal blushed. "If only that were true…" he said a little sadly.

====================

A few days after the party at the chief inspector's, Suzume made an unexpected appearance at Penelope's house to extend an invitation to dinner.

"It's a thank you dinner for you and Fei, and Sal, of course, for all you have done for me. You were so kind to lend us your house for all those weeks when I was preparing and to come and support me. I really will never forget it." she said.

Penelope smiled and waved away her thanks.

"It's no bother at all. We were just delighted you were able to do so well. And if you like, we can do the same next time. I believe you have the final tournament in two months, right?"

Suzume nodded. "Yes, that's right. That's very kind of you again. I think it was the atmosphere here that allowed me to concentrate. And all your food too. It was like those camps the professionals go to in the West when they are preparing for big matches. It made a difference for me."

"Well, Fei will be happy to know that she was able to help. I've heard several people in the *shogi* world say over the years that if she had chosen to go professional and not into medicine, she would have done very well. But, *shogi's* loss is medicines' gain. At least forensic medicine, she's not one for helping the living much…" Penelope smiled.

"Yeah, she's much better than she thinks, and she's a wonderful trainer too. I was so lucky she took me under her wing. By the way, there is another bit of news…."

Penelope looked up from the coffee she was making them both.

"Oh?"

Suzume paused, and Penelope thought she looked a bit disturbed.

"Aunt Mari… she's decided to move back to Akita to help my mother. You know we live with my aunt and uncle… and my great-uncle is not well these days. It looks like dementia… anyway he's getting too much for my mother and his wife to look after. And Mari says she can build a studio in the garden and work there just as well as here, so…."

"I'm sorry to hear that. We'll miss her. Although we only met again this year, having her around has been nice. But what about you? Are you going with her?" Penelope asked.

Suzume shook her head and smiled.

"No, I couldn't possibly live there and have a career in *shogi*. I couldn't concentrate with all of them around me for a starter. So Aunt Mari insists I stay here and look after the house and the cat in Kamakura. So I am going to be one of those lonely, obsessed women with a cat…." she smiled. Then realizing what she had said, she blushed scarlet.

"Oh, I didn't mean it that way Penny-*sensei*!"

Penelope laughed. "Don't be silly. You can't be lonely when you have a cat anyway. That's why I have four…."

Suzume smiled. "So, anyway, it's a farewell dinner too."

"When is she thinking of going?"

"I think she wants to go as soon as possible. They've already started planning the studio, and one of the local builders says he can have it ready in a few months. So, I guess it will be pretty soon."

"Oh… OK. That *is* soon."

"Yeah, when she makes up her mind about something, she likes to move fast. She says she has been in Kamakura too long anyway, says she wants a change of pace…. It's strange in a way, her life and mine…."

"Why is that?" asked Penelope, handing her a mug of coffee.

"Well… it was *shogi* that brought her here to Kamakura too. Just like me."

"*Shogi?*"

"Yeah. She came down here to study, not just at university, but also at a *shogi* school, same as me. She also wanted to turn professional at one point… then she gave it up to pursue art. Hasn't played a game since, she says," said Suzume. "God knows, I've tried many times to get her to play with me, but it's like she's taken some kind of vow."

Penelope sipped her coffee.

"That's very interesting… I didn't know she had been that serious about it."

"Mmmm…. well. She has a picture of herself playing I found the other day. She doesn't know I've seen it. She keeps it in her studio. Do you want to see it?"

Suzume opened up her phone and showed her a picture she had taken of it hanging on the wall.

"Well," said Penelope staring at the old photograph. "Looks like *shogi* really does run in your family. I think your aunt said that to me once as well. I didn't realize she was talking about herself. Anyway, when is this dinner? I will see if Fei is free… she usually is in the evenings."

After Suzume left, Penelope sat staring out at her vegetable garden, lost in thought for nearly an hour. Then, she got up, poured herself a glass of tea, and went and sat on the little wooden verandah with her feet propped up on the stone underneath it.

She looked up into the clear autumn sky, and felt a wave of loneliness wash over her. She thought of Suzume, and how she really needed someone to look after her if her aunt was going away.

And then it all made sense. A wave of understanding passed through her like an electric current, like when you opened a long-locked safe by finally stumbling on the correct combination and the door just opened like by magic. It felt like an enormous jigsaw puzzle just slotting itself into place with a series of satisfying *shogi*-like clicks.

There it was - the whole sordid, evil picture. Even in the warmth of the sun on her verandah, she shuddered.

She needed to talk to Yamashita and Sal, but the sheer certainty of what had suddenly presented itself to her made her in no doubt. Now she would need to act, to confirm what she knew to be the truth.

A few days later, she called Mari and thanked her for inviting them to dinner, which Mari suggested take place the following week.

"Do you mind if I bring a friend, apart from Fei and Sal?" she asked.

There was a pause at the end of the line, and then Mari cheerfully asked her,

"Sure, of course. So... Penny-*sensei*... is this a *male* friend?"

"Actually, yes. It is."

Chapter 19.

The Protecting Bird

"I love these old homes up here in the hills. If I could afford one here, I would have never bought one in Nagano…" said Sal as the four of them waited outside Mari and Suzume's house the following evening.

"Yeah, they're lovely," agreed Fei. "It's so peaceful and quiet in this area."

"I thought you liked where we live?" said Penelope.

"I do. It's just the neighbors are, well…."

"Wonderful," aid Penelope.

The door opened, and Mari stood smiling in front of them.

"Why, hello all," she said cheerily.

"Hello, Mari," said Penelope. "This is my friend, Yamashita Eiji."

Mari and Yamashita exchanged polite bows.

"Nice to meet you… Yamashita-san. Haven't we met before?"

Yamashita smiled. "Actually, we have. We met at the Suwamoto moon-viewing party… and I was at your niece's *shogi* tournament a few months ago. Where we had the unfortunate incident… you remember me now?" he said.

"Oh yes! Now I remember you. You made that speech to everyone. I remember now…." she said, smiling slyly at Penelope.

"Anyway, do come in and have a drink."

They all came into the house and sat down in the living room where Suzume soon appeared bearing a tray of champagne flutes.

"Well, isn't this lovely," said Junko as she came into the room and greeted everyone. "Would you like a drink, Penny-*sensei*?" she said, noticing that neither Penelope nor the chief inspector had glasses in their hands.

"No, not just at the moment," said Penny, with a serious air. "Actually, the inspector and I have something we would like to tell you. All of you, in fact."

Mari sat down on the sofa opposite Penelope with a broad smile.

"Oh… this is so exciting. Please tell us your news, Penny-*sensei*."

Fei and Sal exchanged glances and looked at the floor, and Mari glanced over at them.

"Oh… this is good news, I hope…" she said in a slightly worried tone.

Penelope looked at the chief inspector and then at Mari, and there was a long silence.

"It's over, Mari-san," she said quietly.

"I'm sorry? What's over?" asked Mari, staring at her surprised.

Yamashita spoke up now in his quiet but authoritative voice.

"Setouchi Mari-san. I've come here tonight to place you under arrest for murder."

Mari's face suddenly went as white as paper, and Junko sat back in her chair like someone had slapped her.

Suzume's hand flew to her mouth, and she gasped audibly.

"I don't understand," Mari whispered. "What are you talking about? Is this a joke?"

But one look at the face of Chief Inspector Yamashita soon convinced everybody assembled that this was no occasion for humor.

Penelope leaned forward and clasped her hands in front of her.

"I think you were expecting a love story tonight, weren't you, Mari-san? Well, in a way, this is what it is. A love story between a man and a woman that took place a long time ago, but with… shall we say, terrible consequences."

Penelope paused and stared hard at Mari, whose hands were shaking so violently she placed her glass on the table to stop it from spilling, but she said nothing. Junko was also staring at Mari, and Penelope wondered if, at that moment, she finally understood something about her sister that had been hiding in the back of her mind, something that she had always been too terrified to give voice to.

"I'm going to tell you all a story," Penelope proceeded in a calm voice, "and let me warn all of you now, none of this is pleasant. Suzume, you'll need to sit down, I'm afraid."

Fei stood up and offered her a chair, and the frightened girl sat down and stared at Mari and Penelope like she had seen a ghost.

"This is ridiculous. How dare you come into my house and insult my family like this…." Mari hissed, glaring at Penelope and the inspector, who leaned forward and spoke softly to her.

226

"Setouchi-san, we can do this here, or we can do this at the police station. Please tell me which you would prefer. An officer is waiting in a car outside as we speak."

Mari sat up straight at this, and the tone of her voice softened slightly.

"Go on then. Talk. I've got nothing to hide," she said defiantly.

Penelope smiled.

"Very well then. Let me tell you what I believe, and if I have got any of this wrong, you can tell me…."

Mari nodded and nonchalantly sipped her wine.

"Just get on with it," she said. "And then leave…."

Penelope opened her rucksack and took out a large folder.

"OK. Here we go, then. More than twenty years ago, you came down to Kamakura to go to university at Hassei, where you studied painting. But you were also a promising *shogi* player, very promising, actually. That was the main reason you went to university in Kamakura in the first place, so you could attend a *shogi* school here while you were studying. We also found several clippings in some old *shogi* magazines where you had won several tournaments in Akita, as well as later on down here."

She opened the folder and placed a number of photocopies from old *shogi* articles on the big coffee table between them, with showed faded black and white photographs of a young girl in a ponytail holding up various little cups and certificates.

"I was fortunate enough to have Sal dig these out for me from some of the old magazines we found at the house of

Terumoto Akihisa, who became your teacher when you entered his school."

Suzume gasped. "You were a student at the old Terumoto school? With Yasuo's father?"

Mari said nothing.

"Yes, she was," Penelope answered for her. "And she soon became much more than a student, didn't you, Mari-san?"

Mari looked up at Penelope and glared at her.

"In fact, you became his lover, didn't you."

There was total silence in the room for several seconds.

Mari looked at the floor, but you could tell the sudden disclosure of this information had rattled her confidence.

"I don't understand what this is all about. It's all ancient history," she said quietly.

"So you admit you were his lover? That will save us a lot of time then," said Penelope calmly.

Mari looked at Suzume and sighed.

"OK. We had an affair. So what? That sort of thing happens all the time. I was young…"

Suzume looked at the floor, ashamed.

"It didn't bother you that he was married, it seems…" Penelope continued. "But whatever happened, I think one thing is very certain, and that is Terumoto-san was genuinely in love with … Mari-san. But things soon got out of control, didn't they, Mari-san? Because his wife found out about you. She may have found out from the Enamoto's, I not sure… but she found out, and she came home that night and caught you both together."

"Possibly. Whatever. It's none of your business. And like I said, ancient history," said Mari.

Penelope eyed her carefully and waited to see if she would say anything else, but she simply stared into her wineglass.

"And that's when you killed her."

There was complete silence in the room, and then Mari put her glass on the table with a bang.

"I did no such thing. I never touched her."

Penelope regarded her calmly.

"I think we both know you did. You were desperate… and it might even have been an accident. But she died, and then your lover, Terumoto-*san*, tried to protect you, didn't he? And he had good reason too…. So let me remind you how it happened."

She paused and looked at Suzume, who was staring at her wide-eyed with horror.

"It wasn't a very well-constructed plan, and he literally made it up on the spur of the moment, but he had to give both you and him some kind of alibi. So he asked you to call up his *shogi* club and pretend to be a publisher's secretary. The club captain had never heard your voice before or after, so he never knew who it was."

She paused for a moment, and Mari continued to avoid her eyes.

"You then asked him to pass Terumoto-*sensei* a message about a publishing deal, with a fake address for him to go to. He then smuggled you out of his house, or maybe you waited with the body until it was dark, where you had plenty of time to notice that the gold general had fallen from the *shogi* board on the table above her as she lay on the floor. I'm not sure which it was, but you were definitely there. And then Terumoto-san went off to the *shogi* club as usual, where they gave him the message that you had left. He then went all over Kamakura pretending to look for this place which didn't exist, and once he had made sure enough people would remember his face, he went home and pretended to the Enamoto's that he had lost his key…. And then they found his wife's body," she said.

"The only thing was," said Yamashita, interjecting. "The police didn't believe him. That is to say, my boss, Chief Inspector Toyozaki, didn't believe him, and neither did I. Which is why we soon arrested him for murder. And we were wrong about that, not only because we couldn't really prove it, but more likely because he didn't actually do it. He was simply an accomplice. Someone trying to protect someone else that he loved."

Junko, who had been stony silent up to this point, finally interjected.

"This is all total nonsense. Tell them it's not true, Mari-san.".

Mari looked up at Penelope.

"Is that all you have?" she asked acidly.

Penelope smiled calmly. "You don't deny you were his lover, and we also know he had good reason to protect you, don't we?"

Mari looked at the floor, and Penelope looked at Suzume.

"It's always been about protection, hasn't it?" said Penelope, gently. "That's what I felt when I first saw the picture of Suzume you painted. I looked at the bird, which Fei later identified as a Golden Pheasant. Gold… that's a motif with you, it seems. I was wondering though, what that bird was doing in the picture in the first place. And then it came to me…."

She looked up at Suzume.

"It was protecting her."

There was a dead silence in the room again as Penelope waited for her words to sink in.

"Is there anything you want to say to your daughter, Mari-san?" she asked.

Junko gasped, and her hands shook violently, whereas Suzume stared at them both uncomprehendingly.

"She never told me who it was...." Junko whispered hoarsely, looking imploringly at Suzume. "She said it was a friend at the *shogi* club...."

Penelope looked at her with some sympathy.

"That's right... and you, being her elder sister, someone who had protected her all her life... you continued to protect her, didn't you? You knew she was too young to have a child. And she had no means to support one... so.... you volunteered to do it."

Suzume put her hand over her mouth in shock.

"Mama... is this... is this true?" she asked Junko wildly.

Junko's whole body shook violently, and tears began to roll down her plump cheeks. She looked at the floor and nodded.

"We were going to tell you... when you were a little older... after your tournament..." she managed at last.

Suzume stared at her, and then at her aunt, in horror.

"I'm... your daughter?" she stammered.

Mari looked up at her, her eyes emotionless.

"Yes. I'm so sorry. I couldn't tell you...."

Suzume gasped and burst into tears, and there was silence for a while, broken only by the sound of sobbing.

"And now, we need to move on to the rest of the story," said Penelope. "Because this is not just a love story. It's a story of protection, like I said. Junko-san protected her sister and her child, Terumoto protected Mari and their unborn child, and Mari-san… she would protect Terumoto-san, her lover. The man who had gone to jail for her. And so, to make it seem like the police had arrested the wrong man, a man who actually had a plausible alibi, she continued to murder and make it look like the same person had committed *all* of the crimes. She knew about the *shogi* piece that had accidentally lain on Akiko's body… I think it had just fallen off the table, hadn't it, Mari-san? No? Well, you noticed it, and so did the police. You made sure that when you killed the Enamoto couple and Watanabe-*sensei*, you left the same piece in their hands. And you knew enough about *shogi* to write the letters, from 'Climbing Silver', an opening where the gold general protects the king. That was for Terumoto-*sensei*, wasn't it? And it was not a message that would be wasted on him. He even describes it in his book, the one he wrote later where he describes the protective nature of the piece in the opening. And so the legend of the *Shogi* Ripper came to be…and that eventually led to the release of the man you loved."

Mari stared at her accuser.

"Terumoto-san never wrote a book about *shogi*. Not to my knowledge anyway…" she stated flatly. "I wonder what else you have wrong…."

Penelope opened her rucksack again and placed the eight notebooks containing the notes for *The Quiet Game* on the table.

"Are you sure about that?" Penelope asked her quietly.

Mari looked at the notebooks uncomprehendingly, and then something like recognition stirred in her eyes.

"Actually, he did write a book. Or at least he was planning to. And in it he goes into some detail about the need for us to protect each other in life, and how that is related even to *shogi*…You missed these when you were in his house. They were on his desk."

Mari stared at the notebooks with horror.

"I didn't kill anyone…" she whispered.

"Good luck convincing a judge of that," Sal interjected.

"I was thinking the same thing," said the chief inspector.

"I don't care what you think," said Mari. "I don't care what any of you think. You don't have a shred of evidence I did those things."

"I have more than a shred," said Penelope. "I have the whole ball of yarn… shall I tell you what happened next?"

Mari didn't answer and stared at the floor again.

"OK. Not playing? Then, I'll tell you."

Penelope tapped her finger on the notebooks.

"Nothing. You stopped. For eighteen years. You'd gotten your lover out of prison, so it was mission accomplished, as far as you were concerned. Maybe you thought that one day when things calmed down, you and he could get married quietly and move away somewhere? Maybe like Akita, where you could raise your daughter together? But… that wasn't to be, was it? Because the one thing you didn't understand, probably because you had no experience of it yourself, was that Terumoto-san actually had a conscience. He knew full well you'd killed those other people to get him out of jail. He *knew* it was you…and he couldn't stand the sight of you after it. So he just packed everything up, sold the school, and left. He not only left you… he left his son, who always hated him for deserting him. And then…"

233

"And then eighteen years later, Suzume turns up. A brilliant *shogi* player, like her father…" said Sal.

"My father?" whispered Suzume, the implications of what was being said finally dawning on her. "My father was… oh my God…" she stood up and fled from the room. Junko stood to follow her, but Yamashita pointed her back to her seat.

"You should hear the rest of this," he said. "It isn't pleasant."

Junko sat down again, and Fei left the room to be with Suzume.

"Are we ready to continue, Mari-san?" asked Penelope.

Again Mari said nothing and continued to stare at the floor.

"So, like Sal said. Suzume comes to Kamakura. She has a rare talent and can stay with you while she gets some proper training at the Okamoto school. It all sounds like a good idea, and, at first, I don't think you had any idea that Terumoto's son worked there as a coach. But when Suzume told you, and you figured out they were a couple, you had to put an end to it, right? I mean… he was her half-brother. Wasn't he? Imagine the shock when she found out she was in an incestuous relationship? What would that do to her? And you, of course, had it in your power to make sure she never found out…."

Penelope paused.

"I think that's what the police call motive. Don't you think?"

"We do," said Yamashita.

"And so the cycle of protection and killing begins again. This time you are killing to protect Suzume… and also yourself. First of all, you don't kill the son. That would lead to someone looking at Suzume and maybe even at you. So you decide to deflect the police by starting the *Shogi* Ripper's reinvigorated killings by removing a threat. A man who knows a lot about the case and has never really given up on investigating it."

"And so you kill Chief Inspector Toyazaki, and once the police are convinced that the *Shogi* Ripper is back in town, *then* you kill the son, who was your main target. Now the killing is linked back to all the old killings, which have nothing, evidentially, to do with Suzume. But in killing the son, you know you have awoken the real sleeping dragon… the man who knows that it was you that was really responsible for all these deaths. Terumoto-san, your old lover. You are well aware that he might go to the police and tell them everything in a fit of conscience, especially to get justice for his son. And so you arrange to meet him at his house. Or maybe you wait for him there after he has gone out to his *shogi* club… his house has no real security and is pretty easy to break into. This is important as you want to kill him *and* ensure he hasn't left anything lying around incriminating you. And you find something, don't you?"

Mari looked up at her amazed, but then her expression quickly changed.

"Like I said, I don't know what you're talking about."

Penelope smiled. "Don't worry about that. The jury will."

She opened her rucksack and took out a tattered copy of the *Shogi Times* magazine.

"I owe this piece of evidence to Sal, who sat down at my request and went through every single page of every single *shogi* magazine from the 1980s until today, not only in libraries but in the enormous collection that both the Watanabe family and Terumoto himself had. He found this one in Terumoto's collection, of course…."

She opened up the magazine to a page marked with a small post-it note. On the double-page spread, there was a large article entitled *How a Master Learns the Game*. Penelope pointed to a photograph of a grinning Terumoto holding open a large notebook and pointing to a game notation he had written. On the other page was another black and white photo of a bookcase lined with similar notebooks, ranging across an entire shelf.

"Terumoto, as you well knew, was a meticulous diarist and quite the notetaker. In the article, it explains how he recorded not only every game he played but every game he studied and also what he did every day of his life," Penelope pointed to the photograph of him holding the notebook. "You can see on the bottom of the page here, under the game notation, is a passage where he also says what he did that day. 'Went to the supermarket to buy things for dinner. 7 p.m., exhibition game at club…'" and so on. Now… Terumoto was very proud of these diaries, which he had kept meticulously since high school. And of course, if he were having an affair, he would have recorded plenty about that as well, including, of course, the name of the person he was having it with…."

Penelope took out a large color photograph of a bookcase.

"This is the same bookcase in his house in Ota-ku, where you killed him. Note how all the books are arranged in the same order as in the photograph taken in the 1980s. All the same books are there, all arranged in the same way, by subject. Except... this shelf..." she paused.

She pointed at the picture of an empty shelf, the same one she had first observed in Terumoto's house during her visit with Sal.

"This was where he kept his diaries. As you can see... they're gone."

Mari glared at her.

"So? Maybe he got bored of them."

Penelope looked at her calmly, reached into her bag, and pulled out an old A4 notebook.

"All except this one...."

Mari's look of disdain was suddenly changed into a look of sheer horror.

"Whatever he says in there is not true!" she shouted.

Penelope looked at chief inspector Yamashita.

"Oh, I don't know about that," said Yamashita, looking at her coldly. "I've read it."

"I've read it too. And so has Sal. It's pretty conclusive. And your name comes up... a lot..." said Penelope. "So... you admit you knew about the diaries, Mari-san? Of course, you did... because you destroyed all the others. Probably in your fire pit outside your studio.... We'll have a look there later...."

Mari buried her head in her hands, but Penelope continued calmly.

"There is another thing, however. Something that perhaps shows you are not the total monster your murders seem to indicate."

She looked over her shoulder.

"Fei? Did you find it?"

Fei reappeared with Suzume by her side. She held a large plastic evidence bag in her hand, which she handed to Penelope with a grim look.

Penelope placed the bag on the table on top of the other papers and the notebook, and Mari looked up at it with a look of wild desperation.

"You recognize this, don't you? Suzume told us you had recently hung it in your studio."

Inside the plastic bag was a large framed black and white photograph of a young Mari, who bore an amazing resemblance to her daughter, and Terumoto playing *shogi*. They were both laughing, and Terumoto was pointing at the board with his folding fan. Penelope turned the picture over, and on the back could see the inscription '#1', written clearly in the same hand as the one in Terumoto's house.

Penelope took another old *shogi* magazine from her rucksack and opened it to a page showing the very same photograph that Sal had found.

"You see, I think this was Terumoto's favorite photograph of you. And I think even after all that had happened... he still loved you. And maybe you still loved him too... So even though you got rid of all the journals, or at least thought you had, you couldn't bring yourself to get rid of this, could you? And so you took it off the wall and brought it home. To remind you of the only true love you probably ever had."

Mari stared sadly at the photograph.

"He was the best person... but he would have understood... for Suzume's sake... I had to... I had to do it...."

Penelope looked at Fei.

"No doubt we will find Terumoto's fingerprints on this. This photograph, which could only have come from his house... which proves you were there, Mari-san. And so there is just one more killing... and this one was not to protect anyone else but you... Taniyama-san, whom you wanted everyone to believe was you... Fei?"

Fei went into the next room and reappeared with a large hunting rifle and another small evidence bag.

Mari gave the rifle a single glance and stared back at the floor.

"Over the last few months, you introduced yourself to him and got to know him, so you knew about his medical condition, I think, and, of course, you knew he was Akiko's old lover. So that night, you gave him a choice. There was no need for him to die a painful death. He could either jump from his balcony, or you would shoot him and stage a suicide... He decided to jump... but not before you pushed this rifle into his chest, where you left a tiny muzzle mark on his shirt. He also must have touched the rifle with his hand, right?"

"There is a partial fingerprint on the barrel, which I just photographed and sent to the lab. And also this..." said Fei handing her the evidence bag.

Penelope held it up to the light.

"A tiny piece of white cotton. Just like the shirt he was wearing..." said Yamashita.

"Trapped by the sight at the end of the barrel, presumably when she pushed it into his chest. There is other DNA, too," said Fei.

"Anything to say?" said Yamashita.

Mari groaned and swore loudly.

Then a voice from behind Fei asked quietly,

"Why did you do it?"

It was Suzume, her face calm but furious.

Mari raised her tear-filled eyes and looked at her.

"What do you mean? It was for you... For you... it was all for you...."

Chapter 20

Checkmate

Despite it being a beautiful winter day, with the sun dazzling on the first snowfall of the year in Kamakura, the atmosphere in the playing hall was tense, and nowhere was it tenser than in the little group at the back of the hall that had gathered to support Suzume as she fought in the final match of the tournament which could make or break her dream to be accepted into the elite ranks of professional women *shogi* players.

As usual, her friends had gotten together once more, and Penelope, Fei and Sal had just been joined by Chief Inspector Yamashita, who always looked a completely different person in casual clothes, so used were they to seeing him in his usual dark blue suit.

"How's she doing?" asked Yamashita as he sidled as quietly as possible to Penelope's side.

"You'd better ask Fei that, I don't know one *shogi* piece from another…" she said.

Fei leaned over to him and whispered. "I think it's pretty even. The tournament is tied, this game decides the winner."

The hall was actually a large meeting room that was usually reserved for the use of companies, especially during the annual report season, but the *Shogi* Association had often met here for important tournaments during the year, and Fei herself had played here on several occasions in the past.

Yamashita nodded, and they all quietly observed the end of the final match.

Once again, the other players were gathered around the two remaining players, and once again, they could see Suzume, sitting with her arms crossed as usual, her face a mask of absolute calm as she waited for her opponent to make her move. The only time she moved herself was when she picked up her own piece to play, and slowly and elegantly clicked it into place on the board. Then she would resume her pose, and a complete stillness would once again descend over her. Penelope thought that, in some ways, she reminded her of a heron as it stood in the shallows of a stream, quietly waiting for a fish to come by.

The last several weeks had not been easy, though.

The media interest in Mari had been explosive, but now a few months had passed, the television and the newspapers had reverted to type and moved on to pastures greener, and Suzume was mercifully no longer bothered by reporters calling them at all hours and having TV trucks parked all around Mari's old house in the hills, which she had decided to keep.

However, Suzume had quietly retreated from this house during the last month, and had stayed with Penelope and Fei again as she prepared for the tournament.

Mari was now spending her days in a detention facility in Tokyo, and the presiding judge was going to announce a preliminary schedule in the next few weeks. Owing to the extremely serious nature of her crimes and the number of her victims, there would probably be a lengthy delay while the prosecution and defense teams prepared their cases, but as she had now made a full confession, it was likely that the proceedings would not be drawn out.

Mari's elder sister Junko had been hospitalized for a week with severe stress and heart problems, but she also had now returned to Akita. She had repeatedly asked Suzume to join her there, however, the young woman had stuck to her guns about her *shogi* dreams and decided to remain in Kamakura for the foreseeable future.

Sal had gone back to his work and his other writing projects. He had been singled out for particular praise by the police department for his role in bringing the killer to justice, and the chief inspector had recommended both he and Penelope for a citizen's award, which both of them had declined. For them, it was enough to see the matter finally brought to a conclusion, and in any case, there was no need to stir up any more unpleasant memories for Suzume. There would be enough of that when the verdict was read, and the inevitable death sentence was given to a woman who, for all her viciousness, was, after all, her mother. That was a fact they all knew Suzume kept buried in her heart.

As they reflected on the case, one thing that had shocked and surprised Sal especially was how Penelope had conducted herself that night when they had confronted Mari with her crimes. Although both he and Fei had known the details of what would happen that night, neither was expecting the dangerous little game of bluff that Penelope had decided to engage in, which had resulted in Mari's confession once she believed the jig was up.

The first thing Sal had done when Mari had been escorted out of the house by the uniformed police waiting outside, was to take Penelope aside and talk to her.

"You know… that was a pretty scary moment," he said.

"Which moment," asked Penelope, who was wiping the sweat from her brow with a handkerchief.

Sal pointed to the old notebook on the table in front of her.

"Oh… that moment," she said with a slight smile.

"Yes… that moment. Where did you get that?"

"This notebook? I have a pile of them at home. So do you, probably."

"You lied to her. What if she had asked to see it? She would have known it wasn't Terumoto's. There were no notebooks left…."

"Well, she didn't know that, did she?" said Penelope.

Sal smiled and shook his head in amazement. "Remind me never to play poker with you, Penny-*sensei*…."

"Oh, you needn't worry," laughed Penelope. "That's another game I have no idea about."

"And by the way…" said Sal. "How did you know about the picture?"

Penelope nodded in Suzume's direction.

"Suzume had seen it in the studio, and she showed me a picture of it on her phone, and it was the same as the one you showed me in the magazine and which I found in the study, hidden behind the curtain. I asked Fei to go and get it while we were talking. It was obvious that it was the one missing from Terumoto's house. And if it was from there, then it had Terumoto's prints on it."

"What if she had wiped it or something, though? Then no prints right?"

Penelope nodded.

"Oh, she may have."

"What? So there are maybe no prints on it?"

"I didn't say that. My bet was that *if* she did that, which I doubt, then she only wiped the frame... not the photograph inside it. That's going to have plenty of prints on it. All his."

Sal shook his head again and wagged his finger at her.

"And the gun? What about that?"

Penelope shrugged. "That was Yamashita-san. The gun had nothing on it at all. No white thread, no fingerprints, no DNA. But... she didn't know that either. Remember, she wasn't expecting *anyone* to come after her for that or any of the killings. She was a little careless in the end, I think. Yes. She wasn't sure what she had done, and she couldn't quite remember all the details. Did Taniyama touch the gun? Did she wipe it properly afterward? She may have done, but then again... maybe she didn't. Maybe she missed something... Do you see? It's so easy to plant doubt. It's a bit like when you go out and convince yourself that you left the gas on. Everybody makes mistakes...."

"You are a devious woman," said Sal, delighted.

"OK, thank you. I'll take that as a compliment," she smiled.

Back in the player's hall, there was a sudden movement in the crowd gathered around the table where the final two players were. Fei leaned forward, and Penelope saw her smile.

Suzume was smiling too, and then the sound of applause began to fill the hall.

About the Author

Ash Warren is an Australian author who graduated with a degree in medieval history and English literature from the University of New South Wales in Sydney.

After a period of roaming the world with a backpack, he settled in Japan, where he has now lived since 1992. During that time he has written and published widely on language and Japanese Culture, and teaches at a university in Tokyo.

He is the author of *Dark Tea, The Way of Salt: Sumo and the Culture of Japan, The Language Code,* and *Mastering the Japanese Writing System.* (Also available at Amazon and elsewhere.)

He lives with his family in Tokyo with one dog, two cats and has a penchant for chess, sumo, classical music, and talking about politics over too much sake.

The Penelope Middleton Series

The Quiet Game is the second book in the Penelope Middleton series and the sequel to *Dark Tea*.

If you would like to be updated about further books in the series, please go to:

www.arwarren.net

And subscribe!

Printed in Great Britain
by Amazon